FOR THE LOVE OF JAMIE LONG

Carol Ervin

For the Love of Jamie Long
A Novella, Prequel to the Mountain Women Series

CHAPTER 1

Uncle Bert said we should cry no more. Saying this, he'd looked at me, letting me know I must set the example. I was the oldest girl in the house, almost seventeen. His daughters were thirteen, ten and seven. They were my family, my only family, and that day we'd buried our guiding light, my Aunt Sweet. For the past four years, as she lay ill, I'd felt responsible for all of them. I was used to hiding my grief.

I'd seen him cry a week earlier, when the creek flooded our field, surrounding the barn and the chicken coop, leaving our house on an island. He cursed, too, wading through the water to milk the cow and see what he could lift out of the flood, but I didn't think his crying or cursing had anything to do with the flood. At that point, Aunt Sweet hadn't eaten or drunk anything for two days, hadn't spoken or opened her eyes. For two days she hadn't apologized when I changed her dirty nightgown and sheets. I'd always tried to act cheery, as though the mess was nothing at all, but with her lying insensible, I cried. When I opened the door and let her daughters into the room, they cried too. After watching her closely for so long, we knew what was coming.

"Go back to school," Uncle Bert said, the day after the funeral. He'd allowed us to stay home that week so we could sit with her until the end, even though he wasn't sure the youngest, Mary Agnes, should be present for her mother's death. But Mary Agnes cried and carried on when he tried to take her from the room, and eventually he allowed her to lie on the bed beside her mother. None of us girls saw her last breath, for she died in the night, while we were in our own beds. I suppose that was good. I hoped Uncle Bert had been holding her hand. I'd seen him at night, keeping watch like that.

Even on her worst days, Aunt Sweet had insisted we go to school, saying we didn't need to worry, she'd be right there when we got home. For years she'd said, "May Rose, what would I do without you?" I always said, "And what would I do without you?" She was the only mother I could remember. She called me her first child, though everyone knew I was the child of her dead sister. My father had left me with her when I was two years old. She and Uncle Bert had not seen or heard from him again.

I was my mother's only child, and my Aunt Sweet's first, left in her care when she was newly married. This is the story I was told, the explanation of why I never called Aunt Sweetinia Jonson anything but Aunt Sweet, "Answee," in my baby talk. "I thought your father would return, maybe in a few months when he got used to the fact that your mother was gone," she explained, "so it never seemed right to have you call us Ma and Pa."

My father was a traveling, rootless man, a buyer of livestock who'd come into my mother's life during the county fair. Even after they were married, he'd been away weeks at a time.

Aunt Sweet said she was sure my father had grieved deeply for my mother. Something must have happened to keep him from coming back, some deadly accident. She didn't want me to think he'd purposely abandoned me.

I was four when my cousin Margaret was born, and after that I slowly came to understand my real relationship to the woman who'd mothered me. To the new child she was Mama.

She said the baby was my little sister, so for a while I called her "Sissy," though Uncle Bert's spinster sister soon straightened me out on that. "Margaret is not your sister, she's your cousin," Miss Alberta said. "Sweetinia is your aunt, but she's Margaret's mother."

I didn't understand, but I could tell Aunt Sweet was offended in some way. When baby Margaret began to babble "Mama" and "Papa," my aunt said, "May Rose, why not call us Ma and Pa? After all, you're our first child." I could not change my name for her; I'd had her lap and arms and kisses to myself for as long as I could remember. She was Mama to the new baby, but only to me was she *Answee*.

After Margaret, she gave birth to my cousins Leola and Mary Agnes. Then, when I was ten and Mary Agnes was only a year old, Answee began to keep to her bed for days at a time. "The girls and I can manage," she told my uncle, when he wanted to hire a housekeeper. He suggested his sister might move in with them, but Aunt Sweet said *absolutely not!*

That summer my cousins and I played with Mary Agnes every hour that she wasn't sleeping. We were the ones who taught her to drink milk from a cup. We were the ones who taught her to sit on the little potty. In the fall, Aunt Sweet insisted Margaret and I go to school, so when she wasn't feeling well she allowed Uncle Bert to hire a woman to stay with her and take care of Mary Agnes. No one he hired ever pleased her, and he didn't like having strangers managing his house.

When I was twelve he said, "Our girls can do the work as good as any. You tell May Rose what to do and how to do it. I'll help as I can." I studied ahead in all my schoolbooks because I never knew when I would be needed at home. In those days I looked forward to school, but in the months after she died I had a hard time listening to the teacher, and I told Uncle Bert I wanted to stay home and keep house.

"Your aunt wouldn't approve," he said. We were still trying to do everything her way. My cousins and I were shocked when he invited his sister, Alberta, to live with us. Aunt Sweet wouldn't have liked that.

Miss Alberta was 18 years older than her brother, lived 30 miles away, and she'd seldom visited our house. She'd been married, but nobody ever talked about that, and she constantly preached to all us girls that we must not marry but remain virgins for Christ. She tattled to Uncle Bert when she saw me walking home from school with a boy. "Nothing good will come of that," she said. I wanted to laugh. I knew nothing at all would come of that, for I felt years older than boys my age.

Miss Alberta's residence with us did nothing to improve the state of our household, though she constantly commented on it. "I see you're useful," she told me, acknowledging she'd been wrong to object when my aunt and uncle took me in. I nodded when she told me what to do and how to do it, but her instructions were confusing, so my cousins and I kept to our old ways. Miss Alberta seemed happy, watching from her chair, thinking she was in charge.

She was small and thin-boned, with white hair drawn in a severe bun and bits of shaggy white hair on her face. She lived with us for ten months, enough time for her to repeat all her opinions, like she was afraid we hadn't heard them the first time, or she was certain that if we had, they hadn't sunk in.

We weren't the only people she criticized. "No woman should try to look younger than her age," she said after her first Sunday in our church, adding that plain women should wear gray or brown and not call attention to their shortcomings with jeweled pins, ribbons, and feathered hats. A similar rule applied to young girls. "Never pretend to be more than you are," she said. We didn't quite know what we were, but we withered under her judgment.

"I've never been sick a day in my life," Miss Alberta said, commenting on the weekly prayers for sick members of our church. A week later she died, sitting in her usual place where the morning sun warmed the window. Not long after her funeral, Uncle Bert began to talk to us about moving to North Dakota, a state recently formed from the Dakota Territory.

Before we all knew Aunt Sweet was not going to get well, she'd shared his dream of settling somewhere in the Dakotas, where newspapers said there was abundant land for farming wheat or ranching cattle and horses. Uncle Bert wanted to raise cattle, but because our farm could not raise enough feed for more than four or five head, he also worked as a blacksmith.

"We'll wait till the end of the school year, so May Rose can graduate," he said.

We said nothing, but after he said we'd be moving, my cousins crawled in bed with me and cried. There was no question of trying to change his mind and no need to let him see how we felt about leaving everything we knew. "It will be an adventure," I said, trying to console them. I was just old enough to understand that like us, he felt lost.

CHAPTER 2

We traveled separately to St. Louis, Uncle Bert driving a wagon loaded with what he deemed our most necessary tools and household items, while my cousins and I traveled by train with our trunks of clothes and bedding. At St. Louis, he planned to buy a second wagon and horse team and hire someone to drive it north with us.

"Keep to yourselves," Uncle Bert said, when he put us on the train. "If you keep to yourselves, nothing bad will happen."

I looked at him in disbelief. The worst had happened already.

"When you reach St. Louis, ask the conductor for the name of a respectable boardinghouse near the train station," he said. "Wait there. I'll find you."

He estimated his trip with the wagon would take four to seven days. "All will be well. Don't be afraid," he said.

"Don't worry about us," I said, trying to be cheerful, because Mary Agnes was clinging to my hand. Full of sadness, I had no room for fear.

We'd lived in a community where we knew every face, but now we were surrounded by strangers. At the start of our journey, we got lots of attention and offers of help from other passengers, ladies who gushed about my cousins' good behavior and fair

6

beauty, and men who politely stepped out of the way to let us pass on the crowded platforms and in the narrow aisles. I thanked them as I watched my steps, lifting my head to smile at the women, and being careful not to notice men who seemed to be studying me. On layovers, we sat, sometimes dozing, in train station waiting rooms. By the second day, we were numb to the changing scenery, and our fellow passengers gave us little notice. Like us, they were worn down by the lack of rest and the endless rocking of the train cars on the tracks. I hadn't wanted to go, but by the time we reached St. Louis, I was grateful to be there at last.

When I asked the conductor to recommend a boardinghouse nearby, he said, "Don't you girls go no place but to Mrs. Bond's." Already I felt more grown-up, an experienced traveler. Obediently I heeded his words, waiting with my cousins on the train platform while he told a porter where to take our luggage.

"Come along," the porter said. "Directly there'll be rain."

We hurried after him, across a street busy with clanging streetcars, wagons and carts to a quieter side street. Without the conductor's recommendation and the assurance of the porter that yes, this was Mrs. Bond's place, I would have looked for a house with cleaner windows and no peeling paint. When he stopped there, I said, "This is Mrs. Bond's house?"

"She'll take care of you," the porter said, tipping his cap and leaving us and our trunks and cases on the narrow brick sidewalk.

My cousins huddled close. "May Rose," Margaret said, looking anxiously at the shabby exterior. Mary Agnes clung to my hand.

The house had no welcoming porch, just a stone step to a door. "This is what your father told us to do," I said. I rapped loudly on the door knocker, because rain now pelted down.

Right away a woman threw open the door. "Ahh," she said, looking up and down the otherwise empty street. "Gosh almighty! Is you girls by yourselves? Get in here quick or you'll be soaked." She stood back, motioning us into a dim hallway. Our two trunks were still on the sidewalk.

"Margaret," I said, setting down my valise. "Let's get the trunks."

"Don't worry about them things," the woman said. "Hector'll get 'em." She called, *"Hector!"* A boy who looked about Margaret's age rushed past us into the street and dragged a trunk up the step and through the doorway. We watched as he ran out for the second one.

"Now then," she said.

I drew myself up, trying to look older and wiser. "Are you Mrs. Bond?"

She grinned widely. "So I am." Her face was pocked and sweaty, her pinned-up hair was coming loose, and her dress was faded and shapeless.

I glanced past her at a dusty stairway. "The train conductor said this is a good place to stay."

"Bless his heart, so it is," she said. "You pretty things got to be sisters. Is your folks coming?"

"Pa will be here soon," Margaret said, looking suspiciously at the hall floor, which looked as gritty as the train we'd just left.

We edged farther inside to make room for the second trunk, pushed by the boy, Hector.

"All righty," Mrs. Bond said, giving each of us a smile of welcome. "Will one room do? I got one with a bed and a cot."

When I said that room would be fine, she said, "I do my best to keep a respectable house, but we get all kinds of folks here, so keep your door locked, even when you're just going across the hall to the bathroom. And be sure to lock that door when you're in there. If you want a bath, take it in the middle of the day when there ain't so many here."

With a frown, Margaret pleaded: *"May Rose."*

I could see Margaret wanted me to reject Mrs. Bond's house, but where would we go? Mrs. Bond seemed like a decent person, and Uncle Bert had told us to take the train conductor's recommendation.

"I'll pay one day at a time," I said, "for we don't know how long we'll need to stay. I suppose we should see the room first."

Hector closed the door against the rain, leaving us in near darkness, and Mrs. Bond turned a switch, lighting a bare bulb at the top of the dusty stairway. "Hector, you bring one o'them trunks while I show them the room and the bathroom," she said.

"Perhaps we should leave the trunks where they are for the moment," I said.

That pleased Margaret.

"Sure enough," Mrs. Bond said. "You was brought up to be cautious, and that's a good thing, traveling alone and all. You come to the right place. I'll take proper good care of you girls."

We followed her up the stairs, the boy ignoring my suggestion, dragging one of the trunks along behind us. "He's my sister's boy," Mrs. Bond said. "Strong, ain't he, for not being full-grown? Imagine the man he'll make."

At the top of the stairs she turned onto a hallway slightly brighter than the one downstairs, having a window at the end. "Your room's back here by the bathroom," she said, opening a door. "It's more handy, but the hall gets noisy at times, account of the bathroom, you know. Step in and see how nice it is."

The room was a surprise, brighter and much cleaner than the hall downstairs. "I don't put just anybody in this room," she said. "No bachelors, for sure, 'cause lots of them spits tobacco wherever suits them."

Breathing an approving sigh, Margaret said, "It's very nice."

The air in the room smelled a little stale, for its single window was closed, but there were yellow print curtains, a dresser with a washbowl and pitcher and a bedspread that looked clean. Hector pushed our trunk into the room, then left to bring up the other.

I agreed with Margaret. "This will do very well."

"I knew it," Mrs. Bond said. "Have you ate?"

I was more interested in a bath. She instructed me about cleaning the tub and said we would be the only guests at lunch, for the other lodgers were at work. "I'll be in the kitchen should you need me," she said. "If you want, you can eat the late supper with me and Hector." The other lodgers, she explained, were men, and they ate as soon as they came from work.

The house was old and big, with sloping floors that creaked and a toilet that was slow to flush, but in the next few hours I decided Uncle Bert had been wise to tell us to seek the advice of the train conductor, and the conductor had rightly sent us to Mrs. Bond. We'd been without a mothering influence for too long, and we were glad to have her direct us.

The first day we were happy to bathe and change into clean dresses, eat, and rest. Mary Agnes chattered to Mrs. Bond during a lunch of fried potatoes with bits of bacon, telling her about the school and friends she'd left. We'd already told her Uncle Bert was taking us to North Dakota.

"I take it you're motherless," Mrs. Bond said. She smiled sympathetically when we nodded. "Well it's clear you had a good bringing up."

Water pooled in my eyes, for there's nothing more weakening than a sympathetic word when you've tried to be strong for a long time.

On our second day, Mrs. Bond told us we should get out into fresh air, so in the morning we sat in her weedy back yard and took turns reading aloud from my copy of *Evangeline*. In the afternoon Mrs. Bond suggested we take a walk, and she told us the streets where we could go and where we should not. Margaret kept watching for her father, saying he should be here by now, and what if something had happened? He'd planned to take the wagon overland to the river, then a flatboat down the Ohio and up the Mississippi. Margaret's anxious look didn't change when I reminded her he'd said we might have to wait days for him to catch up with us.

When Mrs. Bond learned Uncle Bert didn't know in what boardinghouse we'd be, she sent Hector to all boardinghouses in the vicinity of the train station with a message for Albert Jonson. "Now wherever he lights, he'll know to come here," she said.

By the third day, we were feeling restless but quite at home in Mrs. Bond's house, and she let us help her wash and put away the dishes and sit in the kitchen to pass the time. "Me and Hector is going to a barn social tonight," she said. "You girls should come along."

I said, "All of us?" I glanced from Mary Agnes to Leola. I felt quite adult, but I didn't know if the social would be appropriate for my cousins.

"All ages of kids goes," Mrs. Bond said. "It's my cousin's barn, and he don't allow no liquor. I'll be your chaperone. We can take the streetcar to the end of the line, then we'll have to walk a bit."

Of course we wanted to go. There'd been no socials for us through the years of Aunt Sweet's illness, for Uncle Bert was not interested in such things, and there'd been no question of going alone.

The barn social changed my life. No one should have been surprised, for I was at an age when change is normal, but I was unprepared for its suddenness. At home in Ohio, my exposure to the world had been limited to events with no new or remarkable people. And though our train journey through Ohio, Indiana and Illinois had put us in close quarters with hundreds of travelers, we'd been taught to speak only as necessary with strangers and never to look at them too much. That night, we looked at everyone, and everyone looked back.

I felt transformed. Even as we approached the wide-open barn doors, my heart beat quicker, spurred by the music flowing out into the night. Inside, I felt immediately included in the frivolity, excited by the fast, sweet fiddle tune, caught up in the spectacle of whirling dancers and the thumping of feet in time to the strumming of the guitars. Little children hopped around, old ladies nodded and tapped their feet while young and old bobbed and swayed and swung each other in circles till they were red in the face. I wanted to dance. So did everyone, whether they knew how or not.

Someone grabbed my hand. "Let's dance!" It was Hector. I

glanced quickly at Mrs. Bond. I'd heard boys were supposed to say, "May I have this dance?"

"Go and have fun," Mrs. Bond said, grabbing Mary Agnes's hands and swaying with her in the crowded area beside the dance floor.

Hector's bold move surprised me, because he and I had never spoken, though we often ate at the same table and passed frequently in the hall. I felt embarrassed, going onto the dance floor with a boy so much younger and shorter, but the purpose of a social was apparently to socialize, and I didn't know how to refuse.

"This is gonna be the Virginia Reel," he said, stopping at the end of a line of women and girls in the middle of the floor. "You stand here, I'll be over there." He crossed a few paces to the line of men standing opposite their partners.

The woman on my left said, "Howdy. Are you having a good time?"

"I don't know how to do this," I confessed.

"That don't matter. Being last, you'll get to watch and see what everybody else does. Just step to the music and follow along—you'll like it."

The fiddle started and one of the men in the band called out, "Three steps up and bow to your partner." The woman beside me tugged on my sleeve and I took three awkward steps and bowed to Hector.

"Now three steps back," the caller said, fitting his words in time to the strong beat of the music. I felt better, seeing a few others who hesitated, also new to the dance. But soon I was stepping and clapping, and there was a lot of laughing as a man or woman got turned around or tried to do the "back to back" with the wrong person. There was no stopping for mistakes, we just scrambled on.

I clapped with a happy feeling as I watched the first couple step out and bend politely toward each other, a woman in white, and a sandy-haired man in a blue checked shirt. While we stood in place and clapped, they linked their arms and swung, then left each other to swing the next man or woman in line. Then they danced back to swing together again. By the time they reached Hector and me, I knew to step forward and link my left arm with the man in the blue checked shirt. He was tall, his arm was strong, and his steps seemed more graceful than those of anyone else in the room. I didn't know then, but this was Jamie Long.

Briefly we swung, left arms entwined, then he stepped away and swung his partner and I backed to my place in line. He and his partner then "galloped" in side-steps back to the head of the lines and we all peeled off in opposite directions, coming together to pass under the first couple's bridge of hands. After that, the first couple took their new places at the ends of the lines, the sandy-haired man beside Hector, and his partner beside me. The routine began again with a new first couple.

"Three steps up and bow to your partner," the caller said. Breathing faster, I stepped forward with genuine pleasure, for though Hector was only a boy, he was a sprightly dancer, and I was having fun. When we all bowed, I saw the sandy-haired man smile, not at the partner before him, but at me. He had beautiful light brown eyes, the same color as his hair.

CHAPTER 3

By the time Hector and I were the first couple, I danced gaily with no misstep, reaching out with my right arm to my partner and then with my left for a turn with every man in the line. To keep from wilting under the gaze of the sandy-haired man, I forced a smile for all. This touching of arms was something new, and later I wondered if touching was the purpose of the dance, a device to put men and women in brief contact, with the music making everything seem proper. Before Hector led me onto the dance floor, I'd touched no part of any man but the limp hand of our preacher after each Sunday's sermon. I could not deny to myself how excited I felt, arm in arm with the sandy-haired man.

When the dance ended, I returned to my cousins, exhilarated but hot. They stared like they weren't sure they knew me, eyes wide but smiling. Mary Agnes tugged on my hand. "Show me how to do that!"

The music started again, this time a waltz.

"I've got you for the next reel," Hector said.

I wanted to dance, but not with this boy. "I shouldn't dance again until my cousins have had a turn," I said.

A tall figure edged past me to Mrs. Bond. "Ma'am," he said. "May I have the pleasure?" It was the sandy-haired dancer.

Beaming, Mrs. Bond took his outstretched hand. "Indeed you may."

We watched them glide around the room among the other dancers.

"Alright, let's dance," Hector said to Mary Agnes. His tone said, "Let's get it over with," but Mary Agnes was happy. She handed me her cup, half-full of something cool and sweet. I finished it because my throat was parched.

"He's nice," Margaret said.

Startled, because I was already thinking about somebody, I said, "Who?"

Mrs. Bond and her sandy-haired partner whirled past us, her hand on his shoulder and his broad hand at her waist.

"Hector," Margaret said. "It's nice of him to dance with us."

I turned to see Hector, who guided Mary Agnes in circles near the wall, saying, "*One*, two, three; *one*, two, three!"

Mary Agnes stepped awkwardly, but she picked up the rhythm. Leola shuffled beside me in imitation of their steps. Margaret looked anxious but refrained from doing anything that might reveal her desire to dance.

The floor was a turning wheel of black and white and browns, working people in their sensible attire. I didn't have to search among them for Mrs. Bond and her partner, for his blue checked shirt stood out. Mrs. Bond was a hefty woman but light on her feet. To my eyes, her partner was not just good; he was perfect. I wondered if they knew each other and if they'd danced together before.

The waltz seemed to last forever, and couples stopped dancing before the music ended, including Hector and Mary Agnes. Mrs. Bond and her partner, however, danced on, and as the floor became less crowded, it seemed like everyone who wasn't dancing was watching them. I felt a blush creep up my neck. I wasn't watching them; I was watching *him*.

At the end of the waltz, he and Mrs. Bond went to the refreshment table, then came back to us, carrying their cups. They stood beside Hector and Mary Agnes.

"Did you see me? I waltzed," Mary Agnes said. She reached for the cup in my hand. "I'm sorry," I said, "I drank it. I'll get you another." I hurried away to the refreshment table, wondering if he was watching me. That was silly. He'd smiled at me one time. He'd smiled at Mrs. Bond and my cousins and likely at every woman in the room.

"May I offer you some refreshment?"

It was a man's voice. When I looked up, a man with a large stomach held out a cup of the sweet punch. "Thank you, I should buy my own," I said. I moved to the table, my coin ready, wondering what I might have done had the offer come from the man I couldn't stop thinking about.

As I paid my money and picked up a cup, a deep voice said, "I'll be coming for a dance." I gave a weak nod of my head, for since I'd come to the social to dance, refusing seemed rude.

After that, I danced every number, for someone always seemed to be waiting with an outstretched hand when I returned to our place at the side of the room. My partners were men and boys of all ages, some who merely rocked me side to side like they'd never danced before. Meanwhile, the sandy-haired man was always whirling by, dancing a turn with each of my cousins, and, it seemed, with every other woman and girl in the room.

I danced with Hector again, the next Virginia Reel, for which the sandy-haired man chose Margaret as his partner. When that dance was over and we returned to our places, he held out his hand to me.

"Last dance," the fiddler called. My shoes had rubbed raw blisters on my heels, but I couldn't confess my discomfort, no more than I could miss this opportunity.

Afterwards, I thought we'd probably waltzed. He'd said his name, Jamie Long, and I'd said mine, May Rose Percy. I was barely aware of the music, conscious only of how he swirled me around the room, his hand on the small of my back and my hand on his shoulder, the pair of us so close together I could feel his breath. It was over too soon.

The room grew dim—someone was turning down the flames in the gas lamps. Voices groaned and the crowd began moving toward the open doors. "We'll dance again," he said. I looked into his eyes and smiled. Then I was outside, the sweat of my face and neck drying in the cooler air, hurrying along with Mrs. Bond and my cousins to the streetcar. Hector squeezed into a seat beside me and started to jabber about something. I didn't hear a word.

* * *

The next days were very warm, and by evening the upstairs rooms were so hot we could not sleep. Mrs. Bond had no porch, so like every other householder on the street, she set a few old chairs on the brick walk, and we sat there late into the night, talking softly and saying hello to people who were out walking in the cooler night air.

Ever since the social I'd secretly watched for Jamie Long, though I knew I was now in a city where I might never see the same person twice. On this dark night I could not be sure, but I felt myself growing weak, witnessing the approach of a man with a familiar, graceful stride.

"Why, it's Mrs. Bond," he said, lifting his cap. Then he turned and also tipped his cap to us, saying, "Young ladies, how are you this evening?"

Lamplight from the windows showed the tanned face of a man with laughing eyes and a smile that turned up on one side.

Mrs. Bond greeted him like an old friend. "Mr. Long," she said. "Do sit a spell."

"Thank you, but I was on my way to the lemonade stand at the railroad station. Would you ladies care to join me?"

Mary Agnes and Leola leaped from their chairs and pulled on my hands. "May we, may we?"

"We can all go," he said, looking at me.

"I'm not certain we should," I said. "Mrs. Bond, will you be going?"

"I'm dead on my feet, but you girls go along. Mr. Long will look after you, ain't that right, Mr. Long? I'll send Hector too. Hector?" She peered up and down the street. "Where'd that boy get to? Never mind, you'll be fine. You should get there and back with time to drink your lemonade, say 30 minutes in all. I'll wait right here."

Thirty minutes. Mary Agnes took Mr. Long's hand. He offered his arm. "Anyone else?" Quickly Leola hooked her arm through his.

"May Rose," Mrs. Bond said, "you and Margaret walk ahead so Mr. Long can keep an eye on you."

I would rather have walked behind, nervous to be so on view, though I told myself there was no reason he'd be watching me. Nervous all the way, I was relieved to reach the lemonade stand, and I stepped aside to calm my fluttery breath while he stood in line, buying for us all.

The lemonade was lovely, tart, sweet, and refreshing, and when we'd drained our glasses, Leola and Mary Agnes claimed him once again for our return to the house where Mrs. Bond was waiting.

We thanked him, and he shook all our hands, starting with Mrs. Bond and ending with me.

"He likes us," Leola said, when we reached our room.

"He likes May Rose," Margaret said, pulling off her shoes. "He's after her."

"He's not," I said, though I was still quivering from the press of his hand against mine.

The next day I was conscious only of the pouring rain and the likelihood there'd be no visit from Jamie Long and no evening walk. I'd wanted to wash my hair, but its length and thickness required hours to dry, and that day we had neither sunshine nor a hot fire indoors. Though our plans for the evening were uncertain, I brushed a bit of powder through my hair and pinned it up. Then the rain stopped.

There was no good reason to sit outside that evening, for the rain had cooled the house and Mrs. Bond said the streets were too sloppy. But after the evening meal we sat in the parlor, and she left the front door open. And he came.

"Ladies," he said, standing in the hallway. "I'm sorry to say it's a poor night to walk out."

"You're right about that," Mrs. Bond said. "It's more a night for tea and a taste of something sweet, don't you think?" She lifted a platter of shortbread. "Do come in and sit down. Mary Agnes, scoot over there with Leola and give Mr. Long your chair."

Mary Agnes's chair was beside Mrs. Bond and directly across the small room from me. When he sat down, I didn't know where to look, though I knew what I wanted to see. I tried to hide my interest by passing my glances around the room.

"Thank you kindly," he said.

During Mr. Long's visit, Mrs. Bond quizzed him about his work, his family, and his future plans, so we learned he was working on the docks but intended to travel west or north as soon as he had an opportunity. He didn't say what kind of opportunity. Of his family he said only that his parents had passed away. Mostly he spoke of catching trout in mountain streams, and though I doubted any of us cared about fishing, we were captivated by the exciting way he told a story. Forgetting to monitor myself, I watched him as avidly as the others.

"What a fine time we've had," Mrs. Bond said, when he stood to leave.

"So we did. There's a barn social Saturday night. Will you ladies be there?"

"I'd say we will if it don't rain," Mrs. Bond said.

Whatever was happening to me, I wanted it to keep happening like I'd never wanted anything in my life.

CHAPTER 4

Jamie Long had stimulated our imaginations, including Mrs. Bond's. "He's got his eye on somebody," she said, "and heaven knows it ain't me."

My cousins and I had helped each other wash our hair, which we were now trying to comb dry in a sunny patch of Mrs. Bond's back yard. Twilight was hours away, but I was eager to look my best by then.

"We don't know him all that well," Margaret said. "And he's old."

"Somewhere in his 30s, I'd judge," Mrs. Bond said. "Thirties and forties are the right age for a man to marry. He's exploring his chances, that's clear to me. May Rose, you should consider whether you want this to go farther or not, and if your uncle would find him suitable. If you don't care for him, or if you think your uncle would object, you best walk out with him no more. O'course it could be our parlor visit last night was enough for him to decide he don't want to see you again. If you don't like him, you'll find plenty others interested. My cousin said some's already asked after you, men that's wanting a wife, that is."

My comb struck a snag in my hair. All I'd heard was the possibility that Jamie might not want to see me again. Last night I'd said nothing but hello and goodbye.

Mrs. Bond continued, laughing. "But you know that's a load of nonsense. Jamie Long is interested, surely you got eyes to see that."

I hadn't said a thing about him, though since the barn social I'd thought of nothing else. I didn't need to consider. He was new and thrilling, and I felt I'd always known him.

"It will come to nothing, for we'll soon be traveling north," I said, picking apart the knot in my hair.

"But Mr. Long said he'd like to go north, didn't he?"

"Or west," Margaret said.

"Well, my dear, prepare yourself to give a yes or no," Mrs. Bond said. "He's a lovely gentleman, and we all like him, don't we girls?"

"We do, we do," Mary Agnes and Leola said. Margaret said nothing. I pulled at another snag, too embarrassed to reply.

I held fast to Mrs. Bond's beliefs, for what I knew of courting and the ways of men was limited to the whispers of schoolgirls. I wasn't ready to show my feelings, but I began to think Mrs. Bond was right. I cared nothing for those other men who'd danced with me at the social. Jamie Long had shown his interest; it was time I showed mine.

He came again, that night and the next. Both nights I stepped forward and took his arm for our stroll to the lemonade stand, as though acknowledging my rightful place. Only speak when spoken to, Aunt Sweet had cautioned, so I initiated no conversation. He did not seem to mind—he talked enough for both of us.

Saturday night, he met us at the barn doors and immediately drew me to the dance floor where couples were lining up for the Virginia Reel.

When the reel ended, he seized my hand. "I want every dance with you."

"You must dance with Mrs. Bond and my cousins," I said.

I was taken away by Hector, and after that by other partners, but Jamie claimed me again and again.

On our way home, Mrs. Bond wanted to know if he'd declared himself. "Nothing of the kind," I said, as though she'd said something foolish. For me that night, sleep was a long time coming.

* * *

Uncle Bert arrived the next day. He'd laid over, waiting for a boat to carry him and the wagon and horses down the Ohio and up the Mississippi river to St. Louis.

Hector showed him into the parlor and called us, then hurried away to see if Mrs. Bond had returned from her shopping.

Uncle Bert seemed different, but maybe that was because we hadn't seen him for weeks. He did not embrace us, for that was not his way, but he smiled and peered closely as though assuring himself that we were unchanged.

I did not feel the same, no longer a girl but a woman experienced in train travel, familiar with a few blocks of a big city. I'd danced and enjoyed the attentions of men, and I wanted to be with one of them forever.

"You had no trouble, then," he said, casting a critical eye at the dirty hallway.

"Our room is nice and clean, and Mrs. Bond is a good cook," Margaret said. She'd worried about her father's journey, and now she seemed to be afraid he'd remove us immediately to another house. But of course unless he changed his mind about our destination, we'd all leave soon.

Mary Agnes stood eagerly beside his chair. "We danced," she said.

"You what?"

I had not planned to tell. "Mrs. Bond took us to a barn social," I said. "All the children were dancing."

"You as well?"

I nodded. "The boy who opened the door for you? He danced with all of us. We learned the Virginia Reel."

"All right," Uncle Bert said. He looked tired. "I suppose there was no harm done."

In our room after each barn social, Mary Agnes and Leota had giggled about the excitement of dancing, especially with the handsome Jamie Long. Wisely, they followed my example and did not mention his name or report that not only had I danced with many men, I'd danced with one man half the night.

Mrs. Bond welcomed Uncle Bert with as much enthusiasm as she'd shown for us, and like us, he changed his low opinion of her establishment when she showed him our clean room, and after that a small one for himself. With her prodding, he shared more than he'd told us about the rigors of his trip. Clearly, he was worn out.

"I don't want these girls to walk all the way to Fargo," he said. "I've got one wagon, but it's loaded with tools and such, so I'll need another wagon and team of horses or mules. I'd be happy if you'd point me to an honest man who deals in things like that."

She said she knew just the man.

The next morning he left the house to speak with another of her cousins, who in addition to making wagons supposedly knew everything about the best places to buy harnesses and wagon teams. We all wanted to go with him, but he chose Mary Agnes, saying we older girls should give a wash to his clothes and pack up our own goods because we might be starting our overland journey any day. Because we'd be traveling through territory where natives sometimes conducted raids, he wanted to join a caravan of wagons. Mrs. Bond said her cousin would know about them, too.

Margaret, Leola and I weren't happy to be left with work, and I suppose we were all downfaced, because Mrs. Bond said, "You girls is gonna have a great adventure. I'd sure like to go someplace different."

I didn't want to go someplace different unless it was with my sandy-haired dancer.

As it happened, the next time I saw him was too soon, a few hours later in the downstairs hall. I'd been in the back yard with

Margaret and Leola, rubbing my uncle's clothes on a washboard and soaking my sleeves and the front of my dress in the effort. The dress was an old one of Aunt Sweet's, so faded and frayed I'd thought about cutting it up for rags. Sweat had been running into my eyes, and my dangling hair half covered my face.

I was coming into the hall from the kitchen on my way to the bathroom when Jamie came through the front door. He looked to be accompanying my uncle and cousin. "May Rose," Mary Agnes called. "Look who's here!"

Embarrassed, I rushed past them and hurried up to the bathroom. After that, there was nothing to do but hide in my room. I had three summer dresses, this thing I wore for chores and the two drying on Mrs. Bond's clotheslines. No one came to fetch me. I supposed that meant my cousins were busy entertaining Jamie Long.

I stripped off the wet dress and hung it in front of the open window, then sat on the bed in my shift, ready to cry, angry that I'd been seen like this. Then, curious about how Uncle Bert and Mary Agnes had found Jamie and why he'd come to the boarding-house, I opened the door a few inches and tried to make out the conversation downstairs. Finally I heard goodbyes and the closing of the front door.

Next I heard Margaret's voice, and in a few moments a flurry of steps on the stairs. I was pulling on the wet dress when my three cousins hurried into the room.

Margaret and Leola were each carrying a basket of freshly dried laundry. "You were supposed to come back and help," Margaret said. "Where did you go?"

I took her basket, dumped its contents on the bed and nervously began smoothing and folding. "I had cramps. I'm all right now."

"Mr. Long was here," Mary Agnes said. "He came to see Pa about driving our wagon!"

CHAPTER 5

The possibility that Jamie Long might go north with us made me weak and happy, but I did my best to appear uninterested as Margaret and Leola quizzed Mary Agnes about her morning excursion with their father. He'd left a message at the cartwright's about needing a driver, and when they returned to the boardinghouse, he'd found Jamie Long waiting outside.

I didn't see Uncle Bert again until lunchtime, when we met at Mrs. Bond's kitchen table. I was certain he'd have something to say to me about Mr. Long knowing his youngest daughter, but throughout lunch he spoke only to Mrs. Bond.

"Your cousin has begun repairs to a wagon he'll sell me at a good price," he said. "So I'm grateful to you for the recommendation."

"Ah, grand," she said. "So you'll be staying here for a time, then?"

"It could be a week or ten days, depending. Your cousin gave me the name of a man who will be guiding supply wagons to North Dakota. He also directed me to a seller of draft horses, but I didn't find what I want."

Throughout their discussion, I attended quietly to my bean

soup and biscuits, trying to look empty of thoughts or concerns. Mary Agnes had not been allowed to stay for her father's discussion with Mr. Long, so we didn't know if he might be traveling with us or not. My thoughts were thick as mush.

"I'll surely miss your girls when you're gone," she said. "They've been good company and willing little helpers."

"I'm glad to hear they've helped," he said. "Now this James Long. He's a youngish sort, 30 or so. He knew Mary Agnes. What do you know about him?"

I stirred my soup and kept my head bowed.

"Ah, that would be Jamie," Mrs. Bond said. "He's a lively sort. I know him from the barn socials. He dances with every female in the place."

He frowned. "I see. My daughters too?"

Mrs. Bond nodded. "Don't worry; I been watching out for them. It's my cousin's barn social, and he don't allow no drinking or coarse talk. I was with the girls all the time. Jamie Long is a polite man."

"I see."

Judgment, I thought, would soon fall on me as the person he'd left in charge of his daughters, though he might condemn Mrs. Bond as well. She hadn't mentioned our walks to the lemonade stand, innocent though they'd been, or her belief that Jamie was courting me.

"If you like," she said, "I'll send Hector around to ask my cousins what they know of Jamie Long."

"Please do," Uncle Bert said. "May Rose?"

I glanced up, ready for a scolding.

"Pass the biscuits, please," he said.

I passed the biscuits, and he resumed his conversation with Mrs. Bond. "I'll judge him myself, of course, but anything you can learn would be helpful. Like if he's honest and hardworking. He's applied to drive for us."

"You should come to the next Saturday night social," she said. "Everybody goes, all us common folk I mean, so if you want to find a team for your wagon, that's the best place to get the name of an honest trader."

Uncle Bert was a quiet, solemn man. I didn't know if he'd ever attended a social event, and I couldn't imagine him dancing.

"I'll go if I haven't found what I need by then," he said.

Mary Agnes spoke up. "Us too, Pa? Us too, please?"

"We'll see," he said.

There were no more evening strolls to the lemonade stand, because Uncle Bert did not think it proper for us to sit on the sidewalk, and if Jamie passed by, he did not knock on our door.

Mrs. Bond did her best, in the days leading up to Saturday, to assure Uncle Bert of the innocent climate of her cousin's barn socials, and he'd not grilled me about our experience there. Instead, he said, "In the journey ahead we could be traveling with all sorts of people, so you will have to learn to be discerning. You must be alert to bad people, even if they seem nice. Go nowhere alone, not even to relieve yourselves."

Later my cousins and I talked about how we might know if someone who seemed nice was really bad. The bad person would soon slip up and reveal himself, we decided. Leola named a girl at school who was nice to her but sometimes said bad things. We decided we could also tell by actions, like if they kicked dogs, pushed little kids around or whipped their horses.

Meanwhile, Margaret worried about where we would relieve ourselves on the journey north. "In the woods, silly," Mary Agnes said. Margaret and I were shocked; we hadn't thought about that.

* * *

Margaret was the only one of us who seemed unconcerned about what to wear to the next barn social. I dug into our trunks in search for something that could be hemmed up, because Leola and Mary Agnes were straining the seams of their dresses. I intended to wear the dress I'd worn before, my blue calico. "It doesn't matter what you wear," Margaret said. "You'll have the most partners anyway. And you'll have *him*."

Though she was four years younger, Margaret and I were now

the same size. I tossed the blue calico toward her. "Here, wear it if you like."

"I don't want it," she said.

Margaret and I worked together on alterations for Leola's and Mary Agnes's dresses, but I could tell she was angry. I didn't care about having many dance partners; I cared only about one. Maybe she cared about him too.

At Mrs. Bond's request, Hector had asked their cousins about Jamie Long, and they'd confirmed what he'd told us: he worked somewhere on the river docks, and he'd only recently appeared at the barn socials. Uncle Bert said the next time Mr. Long spoke about work he'd ask the name of his employer.

On the evening of the social, we rode the streetcar as before, this time with Uncle Bert paying the fare. When he took a seat beside Mrs. Bond, Mary Agnes whispered, "Wouldn't it be nice to stay here and live with Mrs. Bond?"

"Get that out of your mind. We're going to North Dakota," Margaret said.

Either way, I'd begun to think something exciting was in store for me. It was a selfish feeling, but I couldn't shake it.

The band was playing a waltz when we entered the barn, and Hector immediately asked if he could dance with me. I looked at Uncle Bert. "Is it all right?"

He nodded. Hector was a smooth dancer, and with his guidance, I was soon enjoying myself. We were in the middle of the room when the waltz music came to an end. "Let's dance the next," Hector said. The floor was still crowded with couples waiting for the music to resume. I could see over Hector's head, but I couldn't see Uncle Bert anywhere. I saw my cousins, though, standing near the open doors with Mrs. Bond. I was about to say we should return to my family when Jamie appeared beside us.

"Miss May Rose," he said. "May I have this dance?"

Soon we were together as I'd dreamed, one of his large hands enclosing mine, the other at my waist. We danced on the opposite side of the room from where my family stood, and maybe he purposely kept me there. The dance wasn't a waltz, but a two-step. I stumbled through it, at times falling against him. After that, the fiddlers played a polka, and though most of the dancers rotated around the room, again he kept us on the far side of the room.

When the band played an introduction to "Skip to my Lou," Jamie said, "It's a reel."

We took our places in line and smiled at each other across the space. Hector stood opposite Leola. Now that the dance floor was empty of all but the two lines, I could search for Uncle Bert. I saw Mrs. Bond at the refreshment table, but I couldn't find him.

When it was our turn to be the first couple, I realized Jamie was singing as we swung together, "Skip to my Lou my darling." Each time we returned to each other from a turn with another partner, he dipped his head toward my ear and sang, "my darling."

I wanted the reel to go on forever, but when it was over I was heated and thirsty. Jamie bought cups of punch and after we drank, we strolled, like so many others, into the cooler night air.

"We'll catch a breeze over here," he said, leading me away from the barn. He stopped in a quieter, darker place and before I knew what was happening, I'd been kissed. It was very quick, a brief touch of lips, the strangest, most thrilling sensation of my life. I said nothing, but as though he knew I'd liked it, he kissed me again, and this time he drew me close.

My head was full of the scent of him, and then quickly, the strong scent of horses. As my eyes adjusted to the dark, I could see we'd come to a field where people had left their teams and wagons. Arm in arm, we walked on through the field until we came to an unhitched wagon. There he released a pin and pulled down the tailgate, then put his arms at my waist and lifted me up. Far away, the music began again, another waltz. Jamie sat on the tailgate beside me and slipped his arm around my waist. We sat that way, listening to the music, our legs dangling, Jamie humming softly. I let him touch my face and kiss my eyelids, and I let him hug me close.

After a while he lay back, scooting into the wagon bed. "Look at the stars," he said, so I lay back too. His hand reached for mine and laid it over his thumping heart, then he turned on his side and laid his hand on my heart. "I'll never leave you," he said, the words I wanted to hear.

I didn't resist what happened next, for it seemed destined to be, a wonderful thing, the revealing of our bodies, more kissing and incredible closeness. Then there were men's voices, and we stopped and lay very still, clinging to each other in the hard bed of that wagon.

Dark shapes appeared nearby, people coming to collect their wagons, I supposed. Quietly we attempted to adjust our clothing. The shapes stopped between our wagon and the next, lifting their lanterns, illuminating a team of draft horses.

"This is what you want," a man said.

"I like the price." That voice belonged to my uncle. "I'll have to look at them tomorrow in the light," he said.

As the men turned around, their lanterns swung over our wagon. Please don't look, I thought. But they did. A man laughed, then my uncle's voice exploded in the quiet night.

"What's this? May Rose, what...?"

I've tried to forget what happened next, my uncle shouting for the other man to go away, pulling me from the wagon then jumping into it, striking Jamie.

"We're going to be married," I shouted. It was what Jamie had meant, wasn't it? When he'd said he'd never leave me? I waited to hear him say it was true, but the only sounds were the grunts of Jamie and my uncle struggling in the wagon, and far away, the distant music and laughter. I had the silliest thought: my uncle would never allow me to dance again.

Jamie jumped from the wagon and I seized his hand.

"Don't you dare run off," Uncle Bert said.

"He's not going to leave me," I said. "Jamie, tell him. Tell him we're going to be married."

"Sure," Jamie mumbled.

"We'll see about that," Uncle Bert said. "May Rose, get Mrs. Bond and your cousins and go back to the boardinghouse. Then I want you to talk in private to Mrs. Bond. Tell her everything that happened here tonight. Do you hear me? Everything. *And you*," he turned to Jamie. "If you try to run off, I'll send the law."

CHAPTER 6

That night I submitted to Mrs. Bond's questioning, and the next evening she and Uncle Bert went with us to a church where Jamie and I were married. On our way to the church, Uncle Bert said, "I hope this is not another mistake." He said I must never tell my cousins of my transgressions.

Of my cousins, only Margaret had shown no excitement about my marriage. I felt bad about that, because we'd shared more with each other than with the younger two, and I wanted her to be happy. "I'm not going away," I said. "We'll travel north together, and I promise, I'll always be near."

It wouldn't be proper to explain my new feelings, but I hoped someday she'd understand.

Jamie seemed nervous, and my uncle had a serious, set look to his face, but I was too happy to be ashamed. Jamie was mine forever, and we were going to North Dakota with my family! Uncle Bert still would not look directly at him, but he'd accepted him as the driver of our new wagon. In time I was sure he'd come to like Jamie and be glad I'd made such a good match.

Jamie and I separated after the ceremony so he could go back to the docks to collect his pay. Walking away, he turned back and sent me a special smile, a promise that for us, everything would be good hereafter. I was united in the eyes of God to Jamie Long. I couldn't get over it.

"Tonight we'll join a company forming at the north side of town," Uncle Bert said. "The wagons will leave before dawn the morning after that."

We had no wedding celebration. In the afternoon Uncle Bert brought the horse team and the newly repaired wagon to the alley behind the boardinghouse. The horses were only four years old, and perhaps not as seasoned as he preferred, so he decided to drive them himself and have Jamie drive our older, more experienced team.

Midafternoon, Jamie arrived and helped Hector carry our trunks to the new wagon. The wagon had high sides, with attached barrels for water and kegs of beans, fat meat and flour. A canvas was stretched over curved wooden hoops to help keep bad weather off anything and anyone inside.

My cousins were excited about the journey ahead, but I was more excited by the prospect of learning more about my new husband. How long would it be, I wondered, before we could be alone again.

He joined us in Mrs. Bond's kitchen for our evening meal, and then she and my family said tearful goodbyes. Both wagons waited in the alley. Jamie helped me to the driver's bench of the wagon he was to drive.

"All you girls will take turns riding on the bench," Uncle Bert ordered. "When you're not riding you can walk or sit inside the wagon."

Uncle Bert got into his wagon, took the reins of the new team, and told them to walk on. As soon as our way was clear, Jamie tightened our team's reins and said, "Get up!" The horses looked back, surprised by this new voice. When they didn't move, he gave the reins a smart slap and shouted, "Get on with you!" The horses started with a jerk, and I grabbed the bench rail as the wagon rocked. As Jamie shouted and sawed the reins for control, the horses broke into an uneven gallop, then when we got too close to Uncle Bert's wagon, they veered to the roadside.

I shouted, "Whoa!"

"Stupid animals," Jamie said, as they came to a halt.

"They'll be fine," I said. Our horses were used to Uncle Bert's gentle hands and quiet voice.

Ahead of us, Uncle Bert halted his team and tied the reins to a fence post, then trudged back to our wagon. "May Rose," he said, pulling the reins from Jamie's hands. "You drive."

"Me?" I'd driven the wagon a few times to pick up supplies at the general store. It hadn't seemed hard, because the horses knew the way.

"Don't tell her what to do," Jamie said. "She's my wife."

I'd never seen my uncle look so fierce. "It's my wagon," he said. "Until you learn to handle these horses, May Rose will drive."

"Then I'll walk," Jamie said. Humiliation and anger showed in the set of his mouth.

I put a hand on his arm, wanting to make everything right. "Jamie, it's only that the horses know me. They'll get used to you, too."

Ignoring me, Jamie jumped to the ground. Uncle Bert motioned to Margaret to ride with me. After our wagons moved off I didn't see Jamie again until long after we'd reached the campground of the company we were to join. Uncle Bert unharnessed our horses and Margaret and I hobbled them in a field where they could graze. Dispirited, I walked with her to the spot where Uncle Bert was setting up our campsite. Finally I saw Jamie approaching on the road we'd traveled from town. I ran to meet him.

He spared no words. "May Rose, we're going. Get what you can carry."

"Going?" Of course we were going. "Oh," I said, realizing what he meant. *Oh no.*

"I'll not work for him or go north with him. He never gave me a chance."

"Wait till he knows you better. You'll get to know him, too. He's a fair man, and he'll respect you, as I do."

The look on Jamie's face was unforgiving. "If you want to be my wife, you'll do as I say."

I looked from him to my cousins, who were beyond hearing but standing very still, watching from our campsite. "Where will we go?"

"Someplace better," he grumbled.

This was happening too fast. I looked again toward the wagons where my cousins stood watching. How could I leave them?

Uncle Bert came toward us, wiping his brow. "We'll have a lesson harnessing and driving those horses tonight," he said.

Jamie shook his head. "Me and May Rose won't be going on with you."

Uncle Bert seldom showed his feelings, at least not to us. Whatever he was thinking, he did not show it now. "No? What do you say, May Rose?"

Confused and unsteady, I reached for Jamie's hand.

"Many a fine man has gone to ruin from pure stubbornness," Uncle Bert said.

Jamie looked like he was ready for a fight. "Meaning me? May Rose, get your things, we'll need to be out of here by dark."

"Jamie, it'll be... Jamie... can we sit and talk?"

"Take what you can carry," he said.

Uncle Bert turned away and strode toward the campsite. When I caught up with him I said, "Uncle Bert, I never meant... I don't want to leave you and the girls."

"You made a vow," Uncle Bert said, "but I guess where you want to go is up to you."

I'd made a vow, and I wanted Jamie. I also wanted Margaret, Leola, Mary Agnes, and Uncle Bert.

Take what I could carry, Jamie had said. My clothes were mingled with my cousins' belongings in our two trunks. Choked speechless, I climbed into the narrow space in the wagon and began to sort them out, willing myself, as I'd done so many times, not to falter and faint away, but to keep my mind on the task at hand. Margaret climbed in after me. Mary Agnes climbed to the feedbox and peered in.

Margaret seized my hand. "May Rose, what's happening?"

"Jamie says we're leaving." I pulled my hand away and continued laying out my clothing, my eyes too blurry to see. I didn't own much, but what I had was too much to carry.

"You're leaving? Just you two? Where? Why?"

"I don't know. It's what he wants."

She pleaded. "We have to know where you'll be. Maybe you won't be too far from us. Ask him. We'll find you."

I was used to doing as I was told. Uncle Bert hadn't asked if I'd like to go to North Dakota, and Jamie hadn't asked if I'd like to leave my family. Mary Agnes was crying, "May Rose, don't leave us!"

With moisture building in my head and Mary Agnes blubbering, I had a hard time thinking about what I'd need and what I could fit in a travel bag. I couldn't take bedding or cooking implements—those belonged to the family, and besides, there wasn't room. I stuffed my good shoes in our oldest valise, then folded my black skirt and two blouses, undergarments, two dresses, a shawl and the green wool sweater Aunt Sweet had knitted for me before she was too sick to do anything. In small remaining space I added everything I owned of my mother's— her Bible, her copy of Evangeline, and then the soft bag that held her dancing slippers, white stockings, and a black ribbon. Maybe I'd dance again.

Margaret picked up my coat. "You'll need this for the cold."

I couldn't carry it, and the weather was too warm for wearing such a heavy thing. "Jamie will provide." I hugged her tight. "We'll see you soon, I promise. I'll find you!"

"May Rose!" Leola climbed into the crowded wagon, holding something wrapped in paper. It was a money belt. "Pa says you should wear this under your dress. It's a wedding gift, but he says maybe for a while you should keep it secret. He says if things don't work out, write him care of General Delivery in Fargo."

I wanted to say goodbye to my uncle and thank him, but when I stepped down out of the wagon he was nowhere in view, and Jamie was waiting. As he took my valise I said, "I have to tell my cousins where they can write to me."

He frowned. Finally he said, "Jennie Town."

"Is that in North Dakota?"

"West Virginia," he said.

West Virginia? He marched me away so quickly I could not look back without stumbling. We followed the dirt road back toward the city. In the failing light I clutched his arm.

"We'll be all right," he said, shrugging off my arm. "Wait here." He turned off the road.

"Where are you going?"

He didn't answer. Surely he wouldn't leave me?

"Jamie?"

I heard his feet crackling in the brush. He was gone only a few moments, then he reappeared, carrying his valise. "Left my bag here. Almost couldn't find it in the dark." He pulled me close and kissed me. "Don't worry. I'll take care of you."

We walked on. The scent of wood smoke followed us, then the aromas of coffee and sizzling meat. I hadn't eaten anything since breakfast. At the campground, Margaret would be learning how to cook over an open fire with our new iron kettle and tripod.

The moon rose, nearly full, and I said, "Will we go back to Mrs. Bond's house tonight?"

"While the weather is fine, we'll sleep out."

"Sleep out?" I'd never slept outside.

He stopped and gave me a stern look. "What do you think your family will be doing from now till they reach Fargo?"

"I just thought... I mean, I know when they can't sleep inside, of course they'll sleep out. I guess." Sleeping out was something else I hadn't thought about.

"Did you bring food?"

"I thought you meant I should get my clothes."

"They should have shared with you," he said.

I might have told him then about my uncle's gift, but coming so soon after their argument, I didn't think he'd like it. "I'm sorry, I didn't think to ask. And even if I'd known you meant food, there's little I could carry. We have... my uncle has salted meat and biscuit flour, all in barrels." Jamie had made me leave too suddenly, but I didn't say that.

"It'll be all right. We won't starve if we don't eat tonight. We'll have each other. He kissed me again, a long convincing kiss. "That'll be good, won't it?"

It would be good. We didn't leave the road until we could see the distant glow of the city's gas lamps. Then Jamie tramped down a patch of grass under the trees and we spread our older garments on the ground.

There were compensations for sleeping with empty stomachs on hard ground, for we were young and we were fervent.

CHAPTER 7

I woke in the morning to bird song. The day was not quite light, and Jamie stood over me. "I'm going to work," he said. "You hurry back to the campground and see what you can get from your uncle, like some of them provisions. We could use a blanket."

Confused, I said, "Where will you work?"

"Back at the docks for a few days, to get some money for our trip. Get up and go now, 'cause the wagons will leave early." He hurried away.

In the heat of our night together, Jamie had asked me to unbraid my hair, and now it was a mass of tangles. I searched in my valise for a brush, though I was sure I'd left it behind, for my cousins and I had only one hairbrush, the one that had belonged to their mother. Margaret and I had brushed and braided each other's hair, then done the same for the younger girls. We'd pinned up our braids but left the younger girls' hair in pigtails. There were so many things I was going to miss.

I smoothed down the wrinkles in my dress, then quickly combed my hair with my fingers, pulled it back and tied it with my mother's black ribbon. Jamie had left his valise on the ground, so I left mine too. Then I stepped to the road and looked for landmarks, so I'd find this place again. Most of the trees along the road seemed to be the same size, except for a giant that might have been the mother of them all. I took a few backward steps on the road toward the campground, trying to fix my landmark in the dim light. Then I turned and ran on toward the campground.

I was too late. In the light of morning, I saw the flattened and soiled grass, the ashes of campfires and the marks of wagon wheels. Far in the distance I saw a single wagon, a sight that gave me the greatest sense of loss. I was tempted to run after it, though I might not catch it until it stopped. And then what?

Jamie would forgive me when I told him about my uncle's gift. Today I'd buy a blanket and enough food to last until he got his wages from the docks. Back at the spot where we'd slept, I lifted my skirt and took a gold coin from the money belt.

I walked on until I came to the streetcar tracks, then waited. When finally the streetcar arrived, there were no passengers, and the driver got out and lit a cigarette. I entered at the back and showed the conductor my coin. His eyes grew wide. "Miss, the fare's a penny, and I got no change for that." When I started to back down the steps, he said, "Go ahead, take a seat, there's nobody will know the difference." Then he whispered, "Put that piece away and don't let nobody see it."

I closed my fist over the coin and held it in my skirt pocket. A family boarded carrying baskets of garden vegetables, and the conductor left me to take their pennies. Outside, the driver stamped out his cigarette and returned to his seat.

I left the car when it stopped at a street I recognized. From there I could get to Mrs. Bond's house, for she was the only person I trusted to see my gold coin. Maybe she'd know what to do.

I passed by her front door and went around to the back, figuring she'd be in the kitchen. "My girl," she said, "what's happened? Did your uncle change his mind? I hoped he might, for we've missed you already."

"They've gone," I said, then hurried to explain when I saw her quick frown. "Jamie decided we should go back to his folks." This seemed the nicest explanation, though not exactly true. Jamie had not mentioned family when he said we'd go to West Virginia.

"Oh, dear," she said. "The girls will miss you so. But now, have you had breakfast? There's bacon grease on the stove. I can fry you some potatoes real quick. Or I can heat the grease and pour it over these greens Hector picked."

"Whatever you have," I said. "I've money to pay." My stomach was empty and my mouth was watering.

"Nonsense, you've paid enough. This morning you're my guest." She heated the grease and let it dribble over a bowl of greens, then set it on the table.

As I ate the greens, she sliced a potato into the grease left in the pan. "Will you be staying a while, then? You and him?"

"We're moving on. He sent me to buy some things for our trip." I pulled out the gold coin.

"My, my," she said. "A gold eagle."

"I don't have anything smaller than this coin, and the streetcar conductor said I should be careful of showing it."

"That you should. The conductor's a good man to say so; there's plenty would've took advantage. I'm surprised Jamie Long didn't think about that."

I didn't say he hadn't given me the coin. "What should I do?"

"We'll take it to my bank," she said. "You'll be fairly treated there."

She gave me a canvas bag to carry and a pouch to put inside for the coins I'd receive in exchange for the gold piece, for she said so many would weigh down my dress pocket and be obvious.

When we left the bank, she took me to a general store where I bought a blanket and bread and enough slices of cured ham for three days.

When she asked where we were staying, I said Jamie would decide. When we returned to the boardinghouse she asked me to sit and keep her company, but I was afraid Jamie might return to our spot in the woods and be upset if I wasn't there. I promised to visit her as soon as I could, though I knew I would not. Her house was too comforting and too inviting, and if I stayed there too long I might think less of my husband's choices. In parting, she gave me a hairbrush, seeing, I suppose, that my hair was in need.

It was well past noon when I stepped off the streetcar and started down the road out of town. Our overnight spot was not far away, but there were others on the road, a wagon ahead, and later, walkers behind me. So when I reached the giant tree I did not leave the road, but went on for a few minutes, then sat on a mossy rock by the roadside as though to rest. As the walkers approached they veered to the other side of the road and seemed to clutch their bundles a bit tighter. I nodded as they passed, but they looked straight ahead. They were an old woman and some children, and I was amused that they seemed afraid of me. I wondered about that.

I'd worried our spot might be visible from the road, but it was not, and I was relieved to find everything in the small clearing was just as I'd left it. The first thing I did was to drop a few small coins from the pouch into my dress pocket. Then I wrapped the pouch in my wool dress and placed it at the bottom of my valise. If Jamie found the coins, I'd say the wedding gift was meant to be a surprise.

To fill the time and keep myself from worrying about the sounds of strangers going by on the road, I spread the blanket on our grassy bed and opened my Bible to the page where the preacher had written our names and the date of our marriage. Then I lay down, and with my hand on that page, I managed to sleep.

Jamie woke me with a kiss and a whisper. "It's a relief to find you've not been disturbed," he said.

He was the most welcome sight, especially the concern on his face. Surprised, I said, "You worried about me?"

"I was told there's a family of thieves sleeps out at times in these woods." He took my hand and pulled me to my feet.

"Let's go. What I earned today will buy us a safer place tonight."

"At Mrs. Bond's?"

"A house close to my work. I've stayed there before."

I unwrapped the package of bread and ham.

"Ah, good girl, you did as I said. Did your folks pester you to go along with them?"

"No," I said.

He tore off a chunk of bread and chewed it with some of the ham while I rolled up the blanket. If he'd chosen to return to Mrs. Bond's, he might have learned where I'd really acquired these things.

"Will we take the streetcar to our new place?"

"We're well able to walk. We should save our pennies," he said.

I admired this sign of thrift, and I decided this was the time to reveal the surprise. "Jamie, we can still go to North Dakota. I have a wedding gift from my uncle, perhaps enough to buy a wagon and a team of our own. Other things, too."

Jamie had picked up our valises and taken two steps toward the road, but now he turned in surprise. "He gave you that much?"

"I think so. It's in my valise. "Do you want to count it?"

"Not here," he said. "If we don't get going, night will catch us."

"Will we go to North Dakota, then?"

"I'll have to think about it," he said.

The long walk to Jamie's rooming house interested me greatly, for I was a farm girl who'd seen almost nothing of the wider world but railway waiting rooms, the backs of buildings along many railroad tracks, and the streets near Mrs. Bond's house. I gawked at the colors and strange clothing of people on the street as well as the fronts of every building.

We passed tall brick structures near the river, factories and warehouses, Jamie said. Then we walked along streets with small shops and sign-covered windows advertising fish and meat, tools, remedies, dry goods, furniture, and services like barbering and shoe repair. At times, delicious scents drifted from outdoor food sellers, but more often I breathed through my mouth to avoid the stink of rotting fish, garbage, outhouses and piles of manure in the streets. I also stopped looking at the ragged, hungry-looking children and the shockingly-dressed women whose sad, painted faces peered expectantly from doorways and edges of alleyways. Jamie pulled me onward, at times protectively drawing me close to his side. With him beside me, I did not fear the dark looks of strangers.

By the time we reached his rooming house the moon had been shining for an hour. Without Jamie saying a thing, the landlord took his coin and gave him a lamp along with a warning that refilling the oil would be an extra charge. Jamie passed the lamp to me and I followed him up a stairway littered with scraps of paper, dust and grit. The night was young, and I'd hoped we might talk about going to North Dakota, but right away he dropped on the bed and went to sleep. I felt a rush of appreciation for my new husband, who'd worked all day and had walked miles to fetch me from our spot in the grove.

Even in shadows, the small room seemed dirty, and I lifted the lamp and inspected its stained walls and dusty corners. A pair of trousers hung from a wall hook and there was a pile of what looked like rags under the bed, along with a covered chamber pot. An empty basin and pitcher sat on a narrow table of rough lumber. Because the room was stuffy and too warm, I propped open the only window with the short piece of board that seemed meant for that purpose.

The bed was narrow with a thin mattress covered by a sheet that did not smell clean. My dress wasn't clean, either, but I took it off and turned it inside-out, then used it for a pillow. I lay awake beside Jamie for a long time, listening to street sounds, waiting for the small drift of fresher air to cool the room, and thinking about my cousins.

In the morning, I woke to a dismal rain that sounded like it had set in to stay. Jamie had lit the lantern and was putting on the trousers I'd seen hanging from the wall hook.

"Those are yours?"

"This was my room. I went off and forgot them."

"I could give your clothes a wash," I said. "The day might clear and they'd dry over a fence or rail if there's no clothesline. Or in time they'd dry in the room."

"There's no need for that," he said. "Use the chamber pot now if you like. I'll empty it out back this morning and tonight I'll bring you something to eat. There's no meals in this house."

My hands were grimy and I had a powerful thirst. "Where do we get water?"

"I'll fetch it from the pump out back. It'll be safer if you don't leave the room without me."

"I need to stay in here all day?"

"It's best," he said. "Time to time there's foreigners stays here. You want to keep away from them."

"Is there a sitting room downstairs?"

"Not for us." Taking our chamber pot in one hand and the pitcher in the other, he said, "The water's safe, leastways it ain't killed nobody I know of."

When he returned, I said, "Will you think about buying a wagon and going north?"

Jamie tucked his shirt into his trousers. "I'll think about it when I'm ready."

I could see I'd offended him. I had a lot to learn about being a wife, but I wanted to be a good one. "If I had a broom I could sweep the room. Do you have soap?" Soap was something else I'd forgotten. As a wife, I was probably not making a good impression.

"No soap at present," he said. "I won't be so tired tonight. I hate leaving you, I do, but it's for the best." He kissed me, then he was gone.

There was no cup for drinking and no soap for washing my hands. To save the water in the pitcher, I held my hands out the window until rain made them clean and cold, then used them to bring water to my parched mouth. I should not feel sorry for myself; my cousins would be adjusting to new ways too.

When daylight brightened the room, I kicked the rags from under the bed and found a shirt split up the back and a ragged pair of long underwear. I hung both out the window to rinse in the steady rain, swiped them around the floor to pick up the grit, then hung them out the window to rinse again.

For the rest of the day I sat on the floor in front of the window and watched people on the street hurry through the rain. I tried to imagine my family's journey, wondering if rain would turn the ground to mud and if the canvas cover of the wagons would keep my cousins dry.

We stayed two weeks in St. Louis before Jamie said he was ready to move on. He rejected my suggestion that we use the wedding gift to travel to North Dakota, saying only, "For now, it's best we go to a place I know."

Disappointed though I was, I had to trust him. I was 17 and he was older and sure of himself, and because even when the money he earned ran out, he never asked for the gold eagles I carried in the money bag under my dress. I felt proud, knowing he trusted me with that small fortune. I believed that when I got older and proved myself worthy, he'd trust my opinions, too.

Every evening he brought back food for our supper with enough left over for the next morning, and the first day he didn't work, he brought soap and carried up buckets of water so I could wash our clothes.

When he was with me, I laughed all the time, but during the long days without him, I felt sad and missed my cousins. Jamie said their life would be harder than ours.

One night he took me dancing, not to the barn social but to a new place, and to my pleasure, he kept me to himself. I was glad, for I was in the arms of the best dancer in the room, the most handsome and the most fun, and I would have been sorry to dance with anyone else.

He had an engaging way of telling a story, and nights when he was not too tired we walked out together and he entertained me with tales of the people and places he'd known in his childhood. He'd done all kinds of work, and even as a youngster he'd helped his father and brother chop down trees and shape ties for the new railroads being built for the lumber mills. I was curious to hear of his family, but he said there was only his brother, now, and he was a rough old fart.

Our journey to West Virginia lasted weeks, sometimes on foot and sometimes by train. We stayed a few days in rooming houses along the river where Jamie found work at the docks but at other times we slept out or slept sitting up on the train. Wherever we were, I was happiest when he was by my side. When we were alone, he sang to me and told funny stories that made me want to see his homeland.

When I asked why he left West Virginia, he said, "I knew I'd meet someone like you."

I wondered what I was like.

He made up stories about our fellow passengers, shocking, wicked stories that made me laugh. Because he took care of everything, I worried about nothing. He was most attentive when we were crowded by strangers, but of course there were times on our travel when we could not be together, such as the railroad stations where there were separate toilets for men and women.

"Sit with women," he'd say, anytime we needed to part. I always heeded his instructions, but one night when we were delayed in a train depot, the women on each side of me picked up their valises and left the bench to board their train. Then two men took their places. These men smelled of liquor, and they seemed bent on annoying me. First they leaned across me to talk, as though I weren't there.

"Please excuse me," I said, trying to get away.

"No, no, stay right here," the one man said. The other grabbed my arm and pulled me down. "Give us a smile, now. You got a pretty smile. Benny, ain't she got a pretty smile?"

"That she do," Benny said. "She's so sweet I think I'll just take her home to Ma."

Both had their heads close to my face when Jamie seized Benny by the shirt collar and jerked him to the floor. By the time two railroad guards stopped him, he'd hit the other man in the nose, pulled him from the bench and punched him in the stomach, then turned and kicked Benny as he was trying to get himself up.

The speed and violence of his attack had frozen me to the bench, but when the guards started to take Jamie away I jumped up and tried to block their way. "Ma'am, move aside," a guard said. Finally I made them understand that Jamie had only been defending me. They let him go, but they could not arrest the two men, because they'd run off.

People in the waiting room had watched all this. I was too embarrassed to meet their eyes.

Sitting down beside me, Jamie said, "What did I tell you?"

"I know, I know. I did what you said, but the women I sat with left, and those men came and took their places."

"You have to avoid things like this," he said.

I didn't think I'd done anything wrong. I was proud he'd rescued me, but it wasn't a story I'd repeat to anyone.

* * *

Aunt Sweet had taught us to respond politely to questions from our elders without being inquisitive or talking too much. As a result, and perhaps because I was naturally shy, I was attentive to the conversation of others but seldom contributed a word. Traveling with Jamie, I didn't have to say anything, because he spoke for both of us, and since he was a good talker, I enjoyed his lively exchanges with the people who sat nearby. He liked people, I could see, and people responded warmly to his friendly manner. Maybe because he seemed genuinely to care about them, they shared where they'd come from and where they were going, along with sad details like bereavement and financial loss. I noted that for all his talking, Jamie revealed almost nothing about us.

I was not tempted to speak until a new group of passengers appeared, a woman with two little girls and a baby in her arms. I'd heard them coming down the aisle of our train car, the baby crying and the woman directing the children to stop dawdling or she'd be stepping on their heels. "Myra, Amelia, stop here," she said. "There's empty seats, don't you see?" She nodded toward the empty bench across from Jamie and me. "We'll sit there."

Jamie had stretched out his legs, and now he pulled them back to let the woman and her children pass. I smiled at the sweet, smooth faces of the girls, who were yellow-haired, like my cousins. The older one pulled herself onto the seat but the younger, who looked to be two or three, needed help, and her mother's hands were full. "Myra," the mother said, "give her a hand, can't you?"

I looked to the mother. "May I help?"

She sighed. "I'd be grateful." The mother was standing in front of Jamie, and he had a slight look of irritation on his face. He'd be grateful to have them settled somewhere else, I knew.

"Hello," I said to the toddler. "May I lift you to your seat?" She turned and smiled.

"Just do it," Jamie said.

Once on the seat, the toddler began to struggle with her sister for space at the window. Ignoring them, the mother deposited her valise on the floor by Jamie's legs and laid the baby on its stomach across her knees. The baby continued to cry. "I'm Mrs. Goldstone," she said. "This here is Henry. I'm glad we finally got a boy so maybe my husband will stop all that nonsense."

I wasn't used to people speaking so frankly about intimate things, though girls at school had whispered about the kind of activity that resulted in babies. I'd been wondering if I soon might not have one of my own, for there'd been a lot of that kind of activity.

Since she'd introduced herself, I had to respond. "I'm Mrs. Long."

"How do," she said. "Besides these girls here, me and my man's got two married girls and a grandbaby on the way, don't you know. And now I been blessed with Henry." She looked exhausted.

Her little girls were fussing and pushing each other in an attempt to get the best place at their window. Jamie looked irritated. "Why not let one of them sit over here," I said. I was thinking I'd take the older one, who seemed better behaved, but the younger child reached toward me.

"It'd be a big help," Mrs. Goldstone said.

I heard Jamie's grunt of displeasure as I placed the child at the window on our side.

Mrs. Goldstone asked, "Is this here Mr. Long?"

"He is," I said. Jamie didn't reply. With a few jolts, the train moved ahead.

Mrs. Goldstone gave a little shriek. "Oh, I'm riding backwards! Sometimes that makes me sick. I wonder, would you change sides?"

I didn't mind which way I sat, because it seemed as interesting to see the scenery behind us as ahead, but I shrugged, because Jamie was staring stubbornly up the aisle.

"Sorry, I shouldn't ask," she said. "You've been right kind."

The motion of the train settled the girls, but the baby continued to cry. "It's his time to eat," she said, unbuttoning the front of her dress and fumbling till she had the baby's mouth in the right place. "Hope you all don't mind." The baby began to nurse with a smacking sound.

Without a word, Jamie left his seat and went through the door at the end of our car. "Sorry," Mrs. Goldstone said, acknowledging his discomfort. "Some men ain't used to the way of things. So where are you going?"

"Jennie Town," I said.

"Where's that?"

"West Virginia."

"Goodness, we're in West Virginia now. I mean, like where? I wonder if that place is near Lewisburg."

I had no idea.

She chatted while the baby nursed. She was on her way to Lewisburg from Kentucky, and her husband was moving their house goods by wagon. "I thought the train would be more comfortable, but these kids has drove me wild," she said.

I told her about my trip west with my cousins, and she praised me for managing them by myself. "This was before you was married?" When I nodded yes, she said, "You must of been real young."

"Well, younger," I smiled. By about six weeks.

Jamie didn't return for a full half hour, and when he did, he pulled our valises from the overhead rack. "Time to go," he said.

Mrs. Goldstone said, "Oh, are we close to Jennie Town?"

He didn't say. "Goodbye, then," Mrs. Goldstone said. "Guess I'll move over. I hope the next folks that sits here is as nice as you."

I'd thought Jamie was everything I needed, but talking with Mrs. Goldstone had widened my hopes and expectations. Good luck in your new home," I said.

"Same to you." She waved.

Jamie led me through the passageway to the next car, where we sat down with a family that talked in a different language and paid no attention to us. "We shouldn't bother with other folks," he said.

This confused me. It didn't seem wrong to help.

The next station was Lewisburg. "We change trains here," Jamie said. When we stepped to the platform, I saw Mrs. Goldstone walking away, clutching the baby and her valise and ordering her girls to step lively. Jamie and I went into the station building.

We waited in Lewisburg three days for a freight train that included a passenger car, because no passenger trains went to Jennie Town. The first two nights we slept in the woods. Jamie's money was running low, and he said we should save the golden eagles for something more important. I wished I could tell Uncle Bert how frugal he was, and how carefully he protected me. I was also bursting with desire to tell someone how sweetly he loved me, but that would have to be our secret.

Our last night, Jamie agreed to find a rooming house so we could wash ourselves and our clothes. I was happy to have a bed and a roof over our heads once more.

Finally we boarded a car attached to the freight train. It was old, with wooden seats, but Jamie said we'd reach our destination before nightfall. Soon we were in the mountains, steep, wooded, and high, with twisty, narrow valleys. The freight engine chugged up the grades, sending out clouds of black smoke and bits of cinders that at times drifted through the open windows. The views, though, were beautiful. I tried to get Jamie to tell me about Jennie Town, the size of it and the kind of houses and shops, but it turned out he knew little about those things. "I got a buddy started a sawmill there," he said. "Told me he'd give me a job anytime."

A friend in a new place sounded good to me. I imagined him with a wife who'd my friend.

CHAPTER 9

I had my first view of Jennie Town late in the day when we hurried off the train to find a place to eat and sleep while there was light enough to see. There was no railroad station, just a shed with a watchman and a platform for unloading freight. There was little to explore in the town, two or three streets of squat, unpainted houses set haphazardly on a steep hillside. A dirt road bordered the town side of the railroad tracks, and a rocky river flowed along the other side. A few children played in the fading light, and men and women rested on benches in front of their homes.

Jamie didn't know where his friend lived, but he quickly found out.

"Gone," an old-timer said, after a spell of coughing.

If this news disturbed Jamie, he didn't show it. "Where about's the sawmill?"

"Shut down," the old man said. "Some of our timberland burned and your friend logged out the rest. Didn't know how to manage, folks says."

Jamie could be good about disguising his feelings, but I saw he was angry. As though only mildly interested, he asked, "Is there a rooming house?"

"Was." The old man bent over, coughing again, and when he came up he nodded toward our valises. "You wanting a place to stay?"

"Just for the night," Jamie said.

For the night? I tried not to worry about what we might do the next day.

"Mable Morgan's got an extra bed," the man said. "She might be able to fix you something to eat. It'd be kind if you'd pay—she's a widow."

"Of course I'll pay," Jamie said.

"Don't take no offense. I say what's needed, 'cause there's always folks who takes advantage. And Mabel's a good woman." The old man stood, walked us to another street and pointed to one of the unpainted shacks.

I smiled my thanks.

"Much obliged," Jamie said.

Jamie took my hand. "It'll be all right."

"I know." We were both weary of travel and eager to be settled, but I began to hope that perhaps when we'd rested he'd think again about North Dakota.

That night Mable Morgan fed us a hash of potatoes and egg, which she fried in grease over a fire outside so as not to heat up the house. The hash was delicious, and the bed was clean, but there was no privacy because her house was a single room, and our bed was beside her own. I was glad not to be on the ground.

The next morning Jamie left the house to see about work, saying it would be all right if Mable Morgan showed me the town. After she doused the breakfast fire, milked her goat, picked bugs off her potato plants and took a pan of water to her chickens, we walked to the shack that served as post office, store, and lounging place for everyone too old to work. The store carried no great variety or number of goods, just a few items on two shelves. Mable Morgan bought coffee beans, likely with the money Jamie had paid. I wondered how she lived, or for that matter, how anyone survived here. Most houses had only a small garden plot and a few chickens.

Since Jamie had gone to look for work, I was curious about what he might find.

"There's only the tannery, now," she said. It's about a mile downriver. My man wouldn't work there—he never did like to take orders from nobody. He stripped and sold Hemlock bark to the tannery, hunted and trapped and sold pelts and hides, and at times he salted fish from the river and shipped it in kegs on the train. He was a good provider."

In other towns I'd become familiar with the reeking odor of tanneries, caused by the bits of rotting flesh that remained on the hides. The stink got into a man's skin and wouldn't wash away, Jamie said.

Midmorning, Jamie returned to Mable Morgan's house. "Hurry and pack up," he said.

"Did you find us a house?" The morning had left me feeling good about Jennie Town. It was a poor place, but the people were kind and helpful.

"There's nothing here but a tannery. You'd hate me if I worked there."

I couldn't imagine hating him, but I supposed he was of the same opinion as Mabel's husband.

"A freight has stopped for water," Jamie said. "It's pulling out to Winkler in a few minutes."

I shook Mable's hand, and she pulled me into a hug. "You're a sweet child. I'm sorry you won't be my neighbor."

"Maybe we can visit."

She shook her head. "It won't be likely. Winkler's a far piece."

"Will we get there today?"

"Oh, yes, you'll be there in a few hours." She and some of the villagers kindly waved us on our way.

The freight train had no passenger car, just an engine, one boxcar with bawling cattle, two flatcars with strapped-down crates, and a red wooden caboose. At the railroad tracks, Jamie stepped aside and had a conversation with the freight conductor, then helped me up the steps into the caboose. Inside, we sat on a bench along the wall.

"This is a favor for you," Jamie said, "on account of I said my wife couldn't ride on an open flatcar."

"Thank you," I said. "I'll thank him too."

"That's been done," Jamie said. "You best not speak to strangers."

Uncle Bert had said much the same thing, and I supposed he and Jamie knew more about the world than I did.

"I'm sorry your friend wasn't in Jennie Town," I said. "I liked it there. Do you know someone in the next town?"

"A few," he said.

"I hope to meet them."

He frowned. "They're not what you'd call family men."

I missed my cousins, and I was eager for a friend, even an old one, like Mabel, though someone my own age would be better. "Is it a nice town?"

He shrugged, like he didn't want to talk about it. "Good as any, I suppose," he said. "There's a church and school and a store."

Bigger than Jennie Town, then, I thought. "Are there rooming houses?"

"We'll have to see," he said.

I wondered if we'd sleep out again, because the slopes of Jennie Town made me think there might not be many flat places of ground for lying down. And would there be wolves and bears in these forests?

The engine was getting up steam. Outside, the conductor waved a flag toward the engineer, then jumped onto the rear platform of the caboose and came inside.

The conductor was a talkative sort. I listened closely for hints of what my life would be like in Winkler, but he talked mostly about himself and his experiences working for the railroad company, limiting his remarks about Winkler to the sawmill and the railyard. "It's a big operation," he said. "Lumber camps all up and down the mountains send their logs to the big sawmill in Winkler. Winkler's the name of the company. Winkler's a company town."

I didn't say anything, but I suppose I looked quizzical, because he said, "That means the company owns and bosses the whole town. Return trip, we'll carry out a load of sawed lumber. All the way to Lewisburg, then it goes east."

The engine slowed and stopped. "Switchback," the conductor said, going to the door. "Stay put."

I watched out the window but couldn't see where he'd gone. Then slowly we backed up onto a different track, and the train stopped again. After a long pause, the conductor came back to the caboose and the train went forward again. "A switchback is a kind of zig-zag for places where the grade's too steep or the curve's too tight," he said.

At last the train slowed and the conductor said we'd come to Winkler. He got out and the train backed up again, then he came back to the caboose. "We unlink the cattle car here," he said. "You might want to get off, 'cause I gotta wait till it's unloaded and the yardman and me agrees about the numbers and after that we'll go on to the lumber dock." He tipped his cap. "Good luck, missus."

I nodded, and he smiled.

Jamie led the way with our valises, and I followed in the cindered ground between the railroad ties, watching my steps while glancing toward the hillside houses. White plumes of smoke lifted from a cluster of buildings along the river. The air was full of explosions of steam, shrills of saws, and heavy thumps from the lumber docks.

We climbed four steps to the platform of a two-story brick building between the tracks and a busy street. A sign across the top of the building said, "Winkler Logging and Lumber Company." Doors from the platform were labeled, "Office," "Waiting Room," "Telegrams," and "Guards."

"Here," Jamie said. "Stay here while I take care of things."

I sat on a bench against the wall, and he set the valises on each side of me.

"Don't…" he began.

I nodded. "I won't speak to anyone." We were the only people on the platform.

"Sorry if I sound like an old woman," he said. "I worry too much."

"Is there a ladies' toilet in the waiting room?"

"I'll see," he said.

He was gone what seemed an endless time, but when he returned he had a job and a key to the ladies' room. The job, however, was not to his liking. It was in a logging camp, and he said he'd be living there most of the week.

I was confused. "We'll live in a camp?"

He held out the key. "There's no places for women in logging camps. Don't worry, I'll take care of you."

He'd get me a room or a house here in Winkler, I thought, and I'd have neighbors and hopefully a friend, maybe another young woman whose man worked in the camps. There could be many like that here.

When I came from the ladies' room, he said, "We'll go to my brother's until I can figure this out. He's a poor host, so we'll go over to the store and see what we can take to eat."

The street was busy with carts, wagons, and children of all ages chasing between them. I gawked at the houses as we crossed, hoping the people here would be as nice as Mabel Morgan and her neighbors in Jennie Town.

The man at the counter gave me a curious glance before addressing Jamie by name. "Well, Jamie Long, is it? Big plans didn't work out?"

Instead of answering, Jamie handed the man the slip of paper he'd brought from the company office. "Set up my account. I'll have one o'them loaves of bread, ten boiled eggs and a stick of beef sausage."

The man wrapped and tied our items with string, then flipped the pages of an account book to a clean one and wrote Jamie's name and the amounts of his purchase.

Jamie stuffed the items in his valise, then took my arm and ushered me from the store. We walked on the boardwalk until it ended, then crossed the street and walked on a path along the railroad tracks nearly to the end of town. Then he led me across the tracks to the river. "This is the fording place," he said. "We'll have to wade. If you got old shoes, you might want to put them on."

"Couldn't we step across on the rocks?"

"We might try, but they get mossy and slick, and you'd be apt to fall. Don't want you to hurt yourself."

I put on my oldest shoes, a pair of brown, scuffed lace-ups. He kept a firm grip on my hand as we walked through the water, while I did my best to hitch up my dress so the hem wouldn't get too wet. With such tender care, I couldn't complain. Besides, I knew he was disappointed. He hadn't got a job at the mill, like he'd wanted, but he was putting a good face on that. I could too.

CHAPTER 10

To get to Russell Long's house, we followed a grassy wagon track between the slope and a little creek that ran through a narrow valley. Jamie said the house was on the other side of the mountain. "It's my homeplace, and I reckon it belongs to me as much as to him. Don't worry, he won't bother you. In fact, he probably won't speak to you, so while I'm gone, just keep out of his way."

"You're leaving me there?"

"I'll be with you tonight, and I'll be back in three days. I got to be at Camp Six tomorrow, ready to work."

I didn't complain, but I must have looked distressed, because he said, "Sweetheart, I figger your pretty little cousins have had worse hardships on their journey to the north, and likely they'll find no nice house waiting for them there. This ain't what I wanted, but you just gotta bear up. It'll work out."

I felt selfish, worrying so much about myself, when I'd left my cousins to face their hardships alone. Of course they weren't alone. They had Uncle Bert, and they had each other.

From that point on, Jamie made my heart light again, for he sang as we tramped along on the shaded, grassy road, songs that made me want to skip and dance. He'd learned his songs and his dancing somewhere, and I wondered if there were barn socials in Winkler. But when I asked, he said, "That place? The church is against dancing as much as it's against cards and drinking, and second to the company, church folks rules the town. 'Course that don't mean the church stops everything. There's places for cards and such where the company don't own."

"But no socials for dancing?"

"None I ever heard of."

"Then how did you learn?"

The light in his face said he was about to speak of sweet memories. "Ma danced with us when we was little and sang to make the music; that's how I learned my songs. She wanted a fiddle, but Pa was against it."

"Your brother danced too?" A man who liked music and dancing couldn't be all bad.

"Not after he got grown. He was clumsy, always was that way. Ma never made fun of him or said I danced the best, but even a fool could see it."

Late in the afternoon we turned off the grassy track onto one which wound upward through the woods. "We'll be there soon," Jamie said. "We're close."

We tramped on a carpet of pine needles through a dark stand of giant trees with mossy rocks and rotting tree limbs, but soon the pines were replaced by a lighter forest of oaks and walnuts, ferns, and a few sunny spots. "This is it," Jamie said, when the path brought us out to a high meadow where the sky reached down to the ground.

Beyond the meadow was a cluster of rough-lumber sheds surrounded by dirt and puddles. Around the sheds, a flock of chickens clucked and pecked, a horse and a goat nibbled on weeds, and a sow rooted in the ground while her piglets fell over each other in their attempts to latch on to her nipples. The animals were not fenced in, but a whitewashed picket fence surrounded a neat cottage, and barbed wire enclosed a garden where corn grew tall.

"This is home," he said. "Or was."

The cottage was also made of rough lumber, but it had an approach of flat stepping-stones, a foundation of mortised rock, a wide porch with a single chair, and an open door. Fragrant wild honeysuckle bloomed on a lattice at one end of the porch.

From what Jamie had said about his brother, I knew not to expect a warm welcome, and I was glad I was prepared, because we did not get it. He came from the house pointing a rifle. Slowly he lowered the gun, glancing from me to Jamie. "What's this?"

Jamie and his brother looked nothing alike. Russell was taller and broader, with gray in his greasy hair and bushy beard, and he peered like he couldn't see well. His trousers were held up on suspenders over a grimy undershirt.

"Brought my wife to say hello," Jamie said. He held my hand.

"Hello," I said.

Russell didn't move from his place on the porch, say hello or look at me, but he lowered his rifle. "Thought you'd gone west."

"This is better," Jamie said.

I knew enough to be quiet and let them talk.

"Russell grunted. "Where you think you're going now?"

"Got a job with Winkler Lumber. In a camp."

Russell said nothing, but his eyes flicked briefly toward me.

"Camp Six," Jamie said.

Russell nodded. "No room for her there."

"I got money to buy a place."

Our money, I thought, my gift from Uncle Bert.

Russell's brows lifted, like he was impressed or surprised. "Got a place picked out, do you?"

"Hoped you know of something."

"Don't know nothing about town," Russell said.

"I don't want town."

"*She* might like it."

He hadn't said hello but at least he'd acknowledged I was there.

"She wouldn't," Jamie said. "And *I* wouldn't. Can I get to Camp Six from here or do I need to go up from town?"

"I ain't sure where Camp Six is, and likely you'd lose your way in the dark, even if you knowed where you was going. You best go back to town while there's light and go up in the morning with the supply train."

Russell's advice sounded good to me. I whispered to Jamie, "Will we rest before we start back?"

He didn't answer. Instead, he said to his brother, "She'll stay here. I'll come back Saturday night and we'll get on our way Sunday."

"Got no place here for a woman," Russell said.

"Her name is May Rose."

Russell's eyes flicked side to side. "Like I said."

"This here is my place too," Jamie said.

Russell walked to the side of the porch and spit tobacco juice. "You might of been borned here."

"I worked with you and Pa."

"Until you was old enough to chase women. Then you left and I took care of Ma."

Jamie whispered, "Pay him no mind." To Russell he said, "I ain't gonna leave her alone in Winkler. She'll keep out of your way. She's an obedient girl and she's used to sleeping out, so you don't need to make room for her in the house."

I was ashamed he'd said that about sleeping out, for until I'd married Jamie, I'd always slept in a clean bed in a decent house.

"Russell, like I said, we'll leave Sunday. You don't have to feed her or even see her. I'll set her up in the corn crib. Don't worry, she won't bother nothing." To me he said, "Next to the cabin, it's the best place, clean and dry and screened so rats can't get in."

His brother said no more, just turned and went into his house. Jamie showed me the outhouse and we splashed off our faces and hands in the water trough. For the times we'd slept out, we'd acquired tin plates, forks and drinking cups, and Jamie turned a handle of the spout feeding the trough and filled our cups. "It's spring water, safe as long as it comes from the spout," he said. "Don't drink from the trough."

"I'd rather go with you," I said. "Maybe get a room in town?"

Jamie frowned. "You're better off here. He just ain't used to people."

I pressed my lips together in a pretend smile and begged no more, because I did not want him to think I was too easily daunted, a young and foolish girl who might cry like an abandoned baby.

"And on Sunday, when you come back, will we find our house then?"

"I'll find it before I come," he said. "I been all over these mountains, though the logging's made everything look different. There's old folks here just waiting for a chance to go someplace better. They'll sell out for good money."

"You'll buy a place?"

"It'll be fine, you'll see."

Half the corn crib was latticed and screened for corn, and the other half was a storage place, with buckets, crocks, pitchers and lumber stacked neatly on the floor and shelves. Onions hung from a nail, braided together by their dried tops. Jamie was right, the room was clean and tight. Here and there, tin had been nailed over cracks, and the one window was tightly screened. The door was screened, too, so there would be cooler air if the nights were hot.

Jamie spread our blanket on the floor and laid our bread, eggs and the beef stick atop one of the barrels. "The camps feed the men real good, so this is for you. Make it last till Saturday."

He reached out and I walked into his arms, and he wrapped them around me and bowed his head to my shoulder. "You're the world to me," he said.

He had a way of making everything right. He gave me a quick squeeze and stepped back. "I gotta go. Give me them gold pieces."

Stupidly, I said, "You want them now?"

"They'll buy us a place, May Rose."

If he worked until Saturday afternoon, when would he have time to locate a house for us? Perhaps this very night, in Winkler. Surely not everyone there was wicked. He'd spoken of a church.

I lifted my skirt and fumbled at the ties of the money belt. "How many pieces do you need?"

"How many? I don't know what a place might cost, so give me all. Likely we'll need things from the store, too. You did a good job of keeping them safe— now we'll put them to use."

I held out the belt, glad to be rid of its bulk and weight. "Will you wear it?"

"The old pouch'll do." The pouch I'd hidden in the valise held seven copper pennies and a silver ten-cent piece. He handed those to me in exchange for the gold pieces from the money belt. Then he tied the strings of the pouch to his belt and pushed the pouch down into a pocket.

"One more kiss," he said. "Make it a good one, 'cause it's gotta last me three days."

After that long kiss, I stood in the corn crib doorway and watched him leave. A few steps away he turned around and walked backwards, waving. Then he ran to the edge of the woods, where he stopped and turned for a last look. I blew him a kiss and he tipped his cap, turned around and disappeared behind the trees. In my mind I pictured him the rest of that day, retracing our steps back to Winkler, likely sleeping out somewhere, and in the morning, getting on the supply train to his camp, then working all day and somehow finding time to provide a house for us before his return. All while I idled here in my choice of shade or sun.

As I folded the money belt to put in my valise, my fingers felt something hard. It was a coin, caught between the edges of the seam, not a golden eagle, but nearly as good—a silver dollar. My first thought was how pleased Jamie would be to learn of it, but the second was a decision to keep the coin secret against some future need, perhaps a surprise for my hard-working husband.

CHAPTER 11

I saw Russell no more that day, and for a while the animals made me forget I was not welcome here. I enjoyed the curious nosing of the piglets, who came to see if I had something for them, then the goats and the horse, who apparently wanted to be sure I hadn't given the pigs anything. I had nothing to give but Russell's store of corn, and I knew better than to bother that. At twilight, the goats and horse lay down in the pasture, the chickens hurried off to their coop, and one by one the pigs trailed up the ramp into their house.

Since marrying Jamie I'd spent my days alone, but he'd always been with me at night. With the animals at rest, the ridge was so quiet I could hear the trills of insects, a light rustling of air in the trees and the drip of water in the trough. Jamie was right, lodging in the corn crib was better than being cooped in a stuffy boardinghouse. Its screen door could not be locked from the inside, but I pushed one of the barrels against the door before lying down on our blanket, telling myself it was only a precaution against bears.

My night was undisturbed, and in the morning I woke to the scent of coffee. I didn't expect there would be any for me. I peeled and ate an egg with a torn-off end of the bread, then hurried off to the outhouse. Later that morning I saw Russell bent over on the other side of the garden fence. I saw him one more time, walking into the woods.

That day, which I imagined to be Jamie's first day of work in the camp, I used buckets in the corn crib to carry water from the trough for washing our clothes, then spread them on the low tin roof of the pig pen, where they dried quickly. In the afternoon, I sat under a tree in the pasture and thought about homey things like cooking implements and bright curtains for the windows of my new house. Not far away, the pigs stretched on their sides, tame as dogs. I thought about all the things Jamie and I would have in our new home. Maybe he'd find a place like Russell's, with room for animals, but close to town.

The next morning a small, covered bucket waited on the corn crib step. Lifting the cover, I found four yellow-green summer apples, bruised from their fall but soft and sweet. I saved the seeds and gave the core of my first apple to the horse, holding it in the flat of my hand so his teeth wouldn't catch my fingers. That day I didn't see Russell at all. In the hottest part of the afternoon, the chickens dusted their feathers in the dry dirt beneath the corn crib. Like the animals, I sought the cooler air and shade of the woods.

The three days without Jamie passed peacefully and more quickly than I'd imagined. I washed my hair and dried it in the sun, then spent a lot of time braiding it and wrapping it around my head, thinking of Margaret. I hoped my uncle would make a home for them in a place as nice as this. He'd told us nothing about North Dakota, so I didn't know if it was all mountains and trees, like West Virginia, or broad valleys and low hills, like Ohio. I needed to write and tell them where they could send letters. Uncle Bert might not write, but Margaret would. Too late, I wished I'd written about our change of place while we were in Jennie Town. I needed paper and a writing pen, and so many things, most of all, shoes. Jamie needed shoes too.

Every day since leaving my family, the new places of our travel had left me feeling lost and uneasy, but on Saturday when Jamie returned to take me from his brother's farm I knew I was near the end of my journey. We had a home, and soon I'd see it.

He was dusty and scratched and wore a new pair of hobnail boots he called corkers. "Pack up, I want to get there before dark," he said. Our valises were packed and ready, and I'd saved him an egg and most of the beef stick. He opened a new but worn canvas knapsack and I put the last of our food in it.

I waited at the edge of the woods while he went to the house to say a word to his brother. "Thank him for the apples," I said.

He returned in a minute, then we started through the woods. "You'll see, you'll see," he said, when I asked where we were going and what our new place was like. He was tired, I could tell, for he'd worked half of that day and trekked a long way to Russell's.

We went back to the road by the creek, but soon turned up a half-hidden path that circled up, down, and around through darkening woods, stepping over fallen limbs and sloshing through wet places hidden under the leaves. He would not let us stop to rest, though when we'd left Russell's there were hours left before nightfall. The woods became quite dark while light was still visible above the trees. Just at twilight we came out to a patch of broom grass surrounded on three sides by woods. "Here we are," he said, walking me around the clearing.

There was a fenced garden, an outhouse and two tumble-down sheds, one that might be a chicken house. A small stone building was set partly in to the hillside, our springhouse, Jamie said. I pointed to a wooden structure near the open edge of the clearing. "Is that a house?"

"That's it. He left everything," Jamie said.

"Who?"

"The old feller. There's a couple o'chickens and some stuff in the garden. He took off with no more'n the clothes on his back, soon as he saw my money."

The old man's eagerness to leave did not make me feel certain Jamie had made a good purchase. He walked me through the grass to the front of the cabin, and there the view took my breath. On the open side of the clearing the land sloped sharply down, and in the distance, the sun was about to drop behind hills that seemed far below our feet.

"There's a railroad track," I said, going closer and shading my eyes to see the narrow railroad track through the sunset glare. The track ran just at the edge of the clearing, close to a drop off, a stone's throw from the front of the cabin.

"It's for the logs. Goes to the camps," Jamie said.

He thought our new home was complete, but I needed one more thing. "Are there neighbors?"

"Not for miles," he said. "Ain't that a relief?"

No neighbors, no pleasant friend. "But your work is nearby?"

"Up the mountain a ways. The log trains and supply trains goes up and down; you can set your clock by 'em."

I had no clock. "So you'll ride the train to work and back?"

"The logs is sent down before my workday is done. But I'll get here, you can bet on it, every night I can, and always on Saturday." He set down the valises and took my hand. "Come take a look at all the stuff we got."

I stood on the small porch, studying the rotted edges of the floorboards while Jamie went inside and lit a lamp. By the light I saw the single room, the heavy table in the middle, a cast-iron stove in one corner and a bed in the other. Implements hung on the walls. "Something smells bad," I said.

Jamie held the lamp below the bed and pulled out a chamber-pot. "It's full," he said. "I'm sorry, I should've made the old man do a couple things. I was in a hurry to get back to you."

He carried the pot outside, but the odor remained, and I suspected it might be the bed.

"Let's sleep out tonight," I said, when he returned with the rinsed pot. He agreed. Tomorrow we'd make everything clean as new.

* * *

Early Sunday morning Jamie pulled the mattress sack outside, cut it open and dumped the rotten straw in a heap in the woods. I made a fire in the cook stove, boiled the mattress sack and hung it across the garden fence.

While I carried water to the cabin and scrubbed every surface I could reach, Jamie sharpened a rusty scythe and cut down the clearing's tall grass for our new bedding. The cut grass smelled wonderfully fresh, but I doubted there would be enough for a mattress. Dried grass was not thick like wheat straw.

"We'll buy straw in Winkler," Jamie said. "Maybe I can bring it up on the supply train."

"When will that be?"

"Next week, maybe. I'll have to see."

"A horse could carry it," I said, thinking of Russell's horse, but Jamie said we'd seen enough of Russell for a while. I supposed that really meant Russell had seen enough of us.

The old man had left his kitchen and garden implements, a bit of oil for his lamp and lantern, a tin of musty-smelling cornmeal, a pint jar of dried beans, and a covered crock of flour with bugs in it. I tossed the flour and its bugs to the hens. I'd counted three hens, all keeping their distance. Behind the shed there was a chopping stump, a hatchet and an axe, and maybe enough wood to fire the stove for a week. He'd laid up no wood for the winter.

We needed so many things, first of all something to eat, since Jamie had finished the beef stick. He'd found a small nest of eggs when he cut down the grass. I cracked them separately, because even in their shells, some smelled rotten. Out of six eggs in the nest, only two were fresh enough to eat, but I crawled under the half-collapsed doorway and got into the chicken house, where I found two others.

In the old man's weedy garden I found two split heads of cabbage and the hills of his potato patch. I dug into one of the potato hills with a kitchen fork and brought out seven potatoes about the size of eggs. While I was doing that I heard a squawk, and when I carried my produce back to the cabin I found Jamie plucking the feathers of one of the hens.

I was sorry he'd killed the hen, but he said it was old and

probably had stopped laying, and we could buy young hens in town. But when? He had to return to the camp the next morning.

"Point me in the right direction and I'll go to the store for a few things tomorrow," I said.

"No, that wouldn't be smart—you'd easy get lost. There's no road, just the railroad track and the path through the woods."

"Does it take long to get there?"

"A few hours. The path is quicker, it's a lot like the trail to Russell's, not bad walking, going down, but not so easy coming back. Saturday we'll go together."

Late Sunday afternoon I saw my first train chug past the cabin. It carried strapped-down crates and one flatcar of men sitting back to back, their legs hanging over the sides. They waved, and Jamie raised his hand and gave a nod.

I asked, "Do you know them?"

"A few." After that, he had a worried look to him. I wondered if the men on the train had homes and families in Winkler. I didn't ask because he seemed tired of questions about that town. I boiled the chicken and potatoes for our supper, and that night we slept in the cabin with our blanket as a pad over the rusty bedsprings.

Several hours before Monday's dawn, Jamie got up to leave for work. He hugged me tight in the open doorway. "If I can come, I'll be home before dark. If you don't see me, don't worry—likely we've worked late and I'll see you the next night. You'll be safe here."

The moon was still in the sky when he walked away, up the railroad track and out of sight.

CHAPTER 12

Alone, I watched sunlight creep into our clearing, first in beams through spaces in the trees behind the cabin. He'd said I'd have so much to keep me busy I'd hardly know he was gone. I missed him every moment, but he wasn't wrong about there being a lot to keep me busy.

Yesterday I'd used a broom handle to pull down the trousers the old man had left hanging from the rafters. They still lay in a heap on the porch. This morning, deciding to see if any might prove useful, I heated water and put them to soak in his washtub.

Later, while I scrubbed the old man's ragged trousers on a washboard, I heard the putt-putt of a small engine and the clack of wheels on rails. Looking up, I saw a utility cart chug by, going up the mountain. Its only occupant, a man in a dark suit, saw me and lifted his hat. I waved, happy to see another soul.

When I judged the old clothes were as clean as they were going to be, I hung them over the garden fence. Then I forked over the grass Jamie had cut so it would dry on the other side.

After that, I tried to make sense of the garden. It looked like the old man had planted haphazardly or hadn't been steady enough to dig a straight row. Pulling aside the weeds, I found onions with dried tops, more split cabbage heads, and runner beans with their tendrils wrapped around weeds as tall as my waist. Because of the beans, I spared those weeds, but spent the rest of the morning bent over a hoe that had a short, broken handle, cleaning out the garden. The corn patch didn't have as many weeds, but the ears were not ready.

If I'd had seed, I might have planted a new row of beans. While I worked I recited our growing list of needs: paper and pen, bean seed, baby chicks or hens, a hammer and nails, lumber or tin to repair the porch and the chicken coop, straw for bedding, coffee, cornmeal, bacon, maybe a ham. Salt. There was almost enough cabbage to make sauerkraut, but I'd found no salt in the cabin. Yeast for bread. Flour for bread. Lamp oil. I wondered if Jamie had given every piece of gold for this place or if he'd saved some. He hadn't said.

I'd eaten no breakfast, so I picked a handful of the plumpest green beans and boiled them and a potato in yesterday's chicken broth. Jamie had said the loggers ate like kings, and I hoped he'd reached the camp in time for breakfast. I was sitting at the table giving thanks for my food when I heard the railroad cart again. Peering from the window, I saw the man on the cart looking toward the cabin, shielding his eyes against the glare of the sun.

In the afternoon, black clouds built up like a tower in the sky and I gathered the dried grass and brought it to the porch, then re-stuffed the mattress sack. The grass made a thin mattress, but it smelled nice. I left the old man's clothes on the garden fence but carried the mattress into the cabin just in time to beat the rain. The storm rolled in from the west, which meant the hard rain drenched the porch, and I had to shut the cabin door and the window and light the lamp.

Being closed inside made me think of winter, the wood and lamp oil we'd need, the warm clothes and boots we didn't have, and the dark days when I'd be shut up here. Life was hard, Aunt Sweet had said, but I thought she'd be proud of me, a grown-up, married woman, managing well. I couldn't wait to show Jamie what I'd accomplished already.

The rain continued, and in the gray light of the cabin's interior I sorted through the old man's cedar box, surprised to pull out two dresses, a petticoat and a long woolen coat. Their owner must have been tiny, for I could get my arms into the coat, but it was an inch short of closing. There was no use to try on the dresses, but all this clothing could be cut up and put together for a quilt. To my list of needs I added sewing materials: scissors, needles, thread. Batting for a quilt or two, flannel for the backing, stout thread to knot the layers together. At the bottom of the box I found a neatly-hemmed square of soft material, a receiving blanket for a baby. It had never been used, and it made me feel sad.

When the rain stopped, I carried water, heated it, pushed the table aside and set the washtub in the middle of the cabin for a bath, so my skin would be soft and clean for Jamie. I smiled as I washed, thinking of the two of us together.

I was drying my hair in the afternoon sun when I heard the log train go down the mountain. The engineer waved, and I waved back. He was a cheery sort of man, I thought. I imagined a wife for him, someone I might get to know, a woman like Mrs. Bond, but younger.

When rain began again, I knew Jamie would not be home that night. To fill the silence, I sang as I sat at the table and ripped apart the seams of one of the dresses from the old man's clothes box, wondering about the small woman who'd worn it, who'd hemmed a baby blanket and sewed the window curtains, now so rotten they shredded at the slightest touch.

I'd buy cloth for curtains to cheer and soften my new home. Yellow, if the store had it.

* * *

Tuesday morning I ventured once again into the chicken coop and found an egg, still warm from the hen's body. The floor of the coop seemed sound, but the roof looked old and tired of leaning in, like it was ready to give way at any minute. Poor Jamie. He'd need a month of Sundays to get us ready for winter.

I was boiling the egg when I heard the huff and chuff of the steam engine coming up the grade. I hurried outside to wave, and the engineer tooted the whistle. I smiled for many minutes after that, but my pleasure came to a sudden end when I saw crows descending on the old man's corn patch. The chickens could feed themselves on bugs through half the year, but they'd need that corn through the winter, and we'd need even more if Jamie bought new hens or chicks. I flapped my apron in the air to shoo the crows away but they went no farther than the top wire of the fence, ready to wait me out.

Uncle Bert had said crows were the smartest of birds, and a good scarecrow should resemble the gardener as much as possible. That would be me. I could not sacrifice any of my clothing, but perhaps they would remember the old man whose pants and shirts were still hanging on the fence. Again I shooed the crows, and this time they flapped away.

Among the broken handles and rusted iron bars leaning in a corner of the woodshed I found a cross of stout sticks with a sharpened, dirt-crusted end. Back in the garden, I stuck the pointed end of the scarecrow frame into the ground and pounded the top with a rock. Finally, I dressed it in one of the old man's shirts and a ragged straw hat he'd left hanging on a nail by the cabin door.

Before I got back to the house, the crows returned to their places on the fence, and I took the hat from the scarecrow and set it on my head. I'd intended to keep myself clean, but I stayed in the garden to discourage the crows. My reward was finding a hammer half covered with dirt among the dead onion tops. Happy about the hammer, I pulled what onions I could, and dug out those whose tops were dead and rotten, then carried two bucketsful to the porch and spread them to dry.

My thoughts surged with the challenges and rewards of this place, and I was eager to tell Jamie what I'd done and what I'd discovered. I didn't intend to confront him with the list of our needs right away. He'd have his own sense of what was most important, and he'd be tired from his day. And he was the better talker; he'd be so busy telling me about his work I might not say anything.

I did no talking that night, because again he did not come home. I told myself it was just as well, because I was too tired to be a good companion, and he must be exhausted too. I sat on the porch until the sun left me in darkness, then bolted the cabin door, prepared for bed, and stretched out on our thin mattress. He'd be pleased about the mattress.

I woke to a bright, cloudless day and a concert of bird song—a whistler, a chirper, a crier, one who trilled and one who barked. I liked to think they were greeting the morning, singing their delight to be alive, awake, and ready for a new day. Maybe from their hidden perches in the trees they'd seen me and were wishing me a good morning as well. Their greetings were drowned out by the shouts of steam and the rumble of the supply train. I'd slept late, but I felt good. Yesterday I'd made a scarecrow and found a hammer.

That morning I explored new places as well as those I'd searched before, and with each small discovery I thought how pleased Jamie would be. Everything seemed important, like the ball of twine, and the crock of rancid grease in the spring house that might prove good for something. I was delighted by the big discoveries: the sawed lumber and a panel of roofing tin I found stacked beneath the chicken house.

Jamie surprised me that very afternoon. I'd stood up in the garden to wave as the log train slowed, as it always did, going down the grade. I held my breath, seeing him crouch in preparation for his jump, then began to cry as he landed on his feet and ran toward me, arms outspread.

Over and over again he said, "I'm sorry I didn't come, I'm so sorry. They work us till dark, then it's all I can do to finish my dinner and fall into my cot."

He was squeezing me so tightly I could barely breathe. "It's all right, it is," I said. After all, he was working for us, doing the best he could. I leaned back to see his face and he kissed my forehead, my cheeks, and the tip of my nose. When I caught my breath I said, "But you finished early today?"

His lips pressed mine, then he laughed, the bright, musical chuckle I loved so well. "Them dumb wood hicks is still at it. The swamper boss sent me to a new team, said I was to tell them when I got there. I figgered I could do that tomorrow 'cause nobody's gonna miss me, and I'll be back in my cot before the wakeup bell." Laughing again, he took the hoe from my hand and leaned it against the fence. "The rest of this day is for me and you."

I forgot about everything. Jamie wanted a bath, so I helped him with that, and we laughed as he helped me with mine, and before I was dried off we were in the bed, and we stayed there until we had to admit we were hungry and we got up and put on our clothes. I had nothing to feed him but string beans and potatoes and no salt for anything, but he said being with me was better than a feast.

Two more days, he said, when he left. Two more days, then he'd come home Saturday on the log train. "The time will go fast," he said. "We'll get used to this."

I didn't want to get used to living apart.

As soon as Jamie jumped from the log train on Saturday he said we must leave at once for town. He'd brought part of his lunch, a slab of roast beef on bread, all for me, because he hated that he was eating so well while I had almost nothing. We should buy as much cornmeal as we could carry and a crock of fresh lard, he said. Those beans would be good with cornbread. Baking powder, I said. Dry beans, because string beans would not last long. Salt. Bean seed. Writing paper, sewing supplies.

We walked the forest path to town because he said it was quicker. I could barely discern a path, but Jamie seemed sure of himself. The only direction I was certain about was that we were going down. The trees were densely spaced, very large and very old, according to Jamie. A surveyor's mistake had exempted this side of the mountain from the Winkler Company's purchase, so weren't we lucky? I agreed, because he was leading me, holding my hand, helping me avoid low drop-offs and supporting me when I caught my feet in the ground vines that twisted everywhere.

Our dark path finally emerged, not onto a street, but to a slope full of the debris of logging, just above the town. With easier footing and sunlight brightening our way, Jamie hurried me along. Saturday was payday, so all the wood hicks would be in town, the pay line would be long, and the store would be crowded with women. I was to go there and pick out no more than the both of us could carry and tell Mr. Ramey to jot it down.

We crossed the river on a footbridge suspended by cables, a little frightening to me because some boards were loose and the bridge swung side to side with our weight. Jamie ran across it like a kid.

He was right, the line in the store was very long, but I didn't mind because it gave me time to sneak glances at the other shoppers and make up my mind about the offerings on the shelves and in the baskets, barrels, and kegs on the oiled floor. The women chattered to each other like old friends. No one noticed me.

The store had everything, not just food, but clothes, garden tools, furniture, shoes and boots. When it was my turn at the counter, I gave my requests to a clerk who looked no older than Mrs. Bond's nephew. Jamie had said nothing about what I should buy, but I was sure he'd appreciate my prudence. Though I was eager to start on our winter quilt, I asked only for needles, thread, and a pair of scissors, then five pounds of cornmeal, a pound of lard and two pounds of salt, a ham shoulder, a tin of lamp oil. My last request was for three sheets of writing paper, envelopes, a pen, and a bottle of ink. These items did not cost much but I hoped Jamie did not think they were frivolous. The clerk assembled everything as I'd asked, then called Mr. Ramey to approve. "Jamie Long's account," I said.

Mr. Ramey frowned at me and my purchases but nodded approval to the clerk.

While the clerk jotted everything on Jamie's account page, I wrote a brief note to my uncle. "We are living near Winkler, West Virginia. Please send your letters here." Then I printed his name and the General Delivery address for Fargo, paid the penny postage and asked the clerk to add my envelope to the mail bag.

The clerk set down my two burlap sacks near the entrance. "Surely you can't carry these very far," he said.

"Oh, no. My husband is here." Through the open door I watched Jamie trotting across the street, dodging wagons. He ran up the steps and paused in the doorway. I picked up one of the burlap sacks but set it down again because he signaled me to wait. I stood back from the entrance while he bought tobacco and cigarette papers and a pair of gloves for work. Then he took money from his pocket and settled with the clerk.

The clerk had distributed my purchases in the bags so they were nearly equal in weight, but when Jamie came back to me he rearranged them, putting the heaviest items in one bag. "Now then, let's go home," he said, swinging the heavy bag over his shoulder and using his other hand to guide me out of the store. He'd made no objection to anything I'd bought, so I felt I'd made wise choices.

We walked slowly along the street, looking into carts and wagons piled with items for sale. While Jamie looked at guns, I went to the next wagon and sorted through used clothing, rugs and quilts. Next we stopped at a box full of newly-hatched chicks. "Three pennies each," the boy said.

I looked at Jamie. I didn't know if he'd given all his wages to pay our store bill, but I still had a few coins. "My apron has two pockets," I said.

He nodded. "And my shirt has two. We'll take four chicks."

I put a chick in each of my apron pockets and he put the other two in the pockets of his shirt, making bumps on his chest that tempted me to giggle. Having seen other coins in his palm, I drew him back to the wagon with the quilts. "She'll take 20 cents for these two old ones," I said. When he frowned, I added, "They'll be filling for two new quilts." I could piece cloth to cover them.

He put one ragged quilt in his sack and one in mine. Then, with chicks wiggling in our pockets and the bags slung over our shoulders, we crossed the swaying footbridge and started up the slope toward the forest path. Before we entered the woods, he found walking sticks to ease our climb. I was happy, not just from my experiences in town, but because Jamie was leading our way.

We prodded our sticks up through the forest floor, the chicks warm and settled in our pockets and the sacks straining our shoulders. "We could use a horse," I said, adding a little laugh so my suggestion would not sound serious. Jamie did not reply.

I didn't know if we could afford a horse; he hadn't offered to say what he'd paid for our cabin, and I had no idea what money remained from my uncle's gift nor any sense of Jamie's wages. Now we had baby chicks but nothing to feed them; for a few weeks I'd have to give them the cornmeal I'd bought for myself, plus scraps, if I had any of those. I knew a horse would be impractical, especially since it would require hay in the winter. Of course if the chicks turned out to be roosters, they'd soon be food. The boy selling the chicks had said he was pretty sure they were all hens, but since everybody wanted hens, I expected he'd say that. Neither Jamie nor I could tell the difference.

I was tired from our trek up the mountain that evening, but Jamie worked until dark. He braced the chicken house roof with a squared-off log I'd found at the edge of our woods, then nailed a piece of tin across the torn places in the tar paper. The chicks weren't big enough to turn out, so that night we kept them in the cabin in a wooden box near the stove. Jamie said the camp cook kept chickens, and he might part with an unused scrap of chicken wire for a pen where our chicks could safely scratch on the ground. "But not until they've got their pin feathers," I said. He acknowledged I was right.

Our sweetest times outside were the ones just before sundown, when we sat on our porch with a glass of cool spring water and spoke of all we hoped to do. He said he loved the sound of my voice reading "Evangeline". As for me, I could have listened to him sing all day. Before he left that Sunday, he sang "Farewell," and we tried to waltz in the lumpy grass.

Farewell, farewell to you who would hear,
You lonely travelers all,

The cold north wind will blow again,
The winding road does call.

"This is a sad song," I said, stumbling in his arms.

"Ma said the best songs have a bit of sadness to them." Jamie's voice grew tender when he spoke of his mother, a wonderful singer. I didn't try to sing with Jamie because my cousins had let me know I couldn't carry a tune.

Sunday afternoon when we heard the train coming up the mountain, he gave me a quick kiss, settled his cap farther down on his head, and ran to the tracks. A flatcar of loggers appeared, sitting on crates and on the deck of the car, and they reached down and helped him jump up beside them. When he turned and sat down I waved, but perhaps he did not see, because he did not wave back. Then the train was gone.

Remembering our hours together filled the next days and nights. He'd admired my work in the garden but laughed at my scarecrow and warned the crows would be back as soon as the ears of corn filled out. I knew that. "If you pick too soon, the ears will mold," he said. I knew that too. There was much to be happy about. Of all the places we'd been in our short, married life, this place was best because it was ours.

Alone again, I cut and sewed pieces for the new quilts. Jamie had said he might not be able to slip away from work, so I should not expect him to come until the following Saturday. Thursday night, however, I woke to a knocking on the door. "May Rose, May Rose. Unbar the door!" We had a feverish hour together, then he was gone again.

The next day was gray and rainy, so the chicks and I stayed inside with a small fire in the stove and a light in the lamp so I could see to make my stiches. My quilt coverings had no special pattern, cut as they were from the goods I had on hand, but I was proud of them.

I'd thought we might go to town the next Saturday, but Jamie had work in mind, a hog lot, and as soon as he jumped off the log train he set to work on it, staking out a space at the edge of the woods to be enclosed with boards and barbed wire and a little house for the weather.

He'd brought no chicken wire, but he had another a present from camp, an entire loaf of light bread. Since I had no flour or yeast, the bread was a delight. Each of our moments together were like cream rising to the top of a pitcher of milk, the best part of everything. I told myself the time without him was a test of character. He said we would not live apart forever.

The little chicks were a blessing, and I guarded them like a mother hen, sitting nearby while they learned to scratch and peck in the dirt. Our two hens were still providing one egg every day, and I had beans and potatoes from the garden, seasoned with a small sliver of ham. I worried about winter.

Jamie was working so hard for us, both at his job and on weekends that I did not complain, the following Saturday, when he left nearly as soon as he got home to go to his brother's house. "I need to borrow the horse so I can haul up some barbed wire," he said. "Chicken wire, too." Russell had a litter of pigs, and Jamie was sure he'd give us one.

I tried not to show how sorry I was to be left alone again.

CHAPTER 14

I had some regrets. In long nights awake, listening to the wind, or rain, or the shrill of night insects, I thought of nights in Mrs. Bond's house when I'd been nestled cozily in bed between Mary Agnes and Leola. At my loneliest times, I wished Jamie and I had been in less of a hurry to do what our bodies urged, for if we'd been more patient and more prudent, we might now be in Fargo with my family. I tried to imagine what they were doing. I hoped Margaret or Uncle Bert would write soon.

The next Saturday Jamie came home in a bad mood. I always knew how he felt about anything, and I partly admired his honest reactions. For myself, though, I didn't know how I'd get through my days and nights if I couldn't look on the bright side of everything.

I did not tell Jamie to look on the bright side, and I agreed he'd been unfairly treated. The camp boss had docked Jamie's pay, accusing him of stealing from the kitchen. "One loaf of bread," Jamie said. "If I'd stayed in camp for the weekend, I'd have eaten a lot more than a sorry loaf of bread."

Maybe he'd forgotten I was baking bread, now. Last week,

along with the wire he'd carried from the store on Russell's horse, he'd brought a twenty-pound sack of flour and a jar of yeast.

He expended the energy of his rage on the hog lot. I helped, holding boards in place while he hammered, and after a while he settled down.

"I'm sorry," he said. "I do kind of hang around the camp kitchen, but that's 'cause I'd like to be a cook someday, and I'm trying to see how he does things. They tell me the cook has the best wages of any man in camp. I've got no chance getting on his crew, though, 'cause he's taken against me. I wasn't stealing that bread, I was admiring it!"

I thought this was odd, for Jamie had shown no interest in cooking when he was home, but I said I was sorry too.

He leaned over and gave me a quick, sweaty kiss. "You bring out the good in me. I know I've a speck of good because Ma said I did!" He laughed and after that his mood improved.

The hog lot included a board fence with a gate and a small board and tin house set up on rocks. We finished it that weekend and looked on our work with pride. That was what life was about, I thought, devoting our days not just to our pleasures, but doing something for the future. "Next Saturday we'll get a young sow from Russell," Jamie said, "one we can breed for litters of our own."

I asked what a young pig would cost but Jamie was pretty sure his brother would give it to us. "I'll say we got a wedding gift coming." He laughed again.

I was happy to hear him say I would be going too. I hadn't been away from the house since we'd bought the chicks, so I was excited about the change of scenery, even if I doubted Russell would be glad to see me. Jamie said it wasn't anything against me; Russell just didn't like women. And maybe he would give us the pig. I wondered if he still had apples. I'd planted the seeds from the apples he'd given me and now had four tender saplings growing in cans.

Saturday I carried the quilt I'd finished, so we'd have a nice pad to lie on in Russell's corn crib. We slept the night there, eating the bread I'd brought along, because Russell offered nothing.

Jamie waited until we were ready to go the next morning to choose our pig.

As I'd feared, Russell wasn't about to give it away.

Jamie said, "I think I'm due a lot more than a pig from our homeplace. Why should you have it all?"

Russell stood his ground. "Where was you when I was patching up and planting all this here? Where was you when Ma was sick?"

Then, seeing the quilt bundled under my arm, Russell said, "I'll take that there quilt for a pig."

Surprised, I stiffened my arm over the quilt, but Jamie eased the quilt away. "It's nice and plump," he said. But when Jamie started to put a noose around the neck of his chosen pig, Russell said, "Not that there. Take the runt."

They had more angry words and I stepped away and tried not to listen, but in the end we went home with the runt. Clearly, the little pig did not want to go, and she did not walk obediently at the end of her rope, and I was distressed at her squeals and the way Jamie jerked the rope and hit her with a stick to make her walk along. Finally, when we were all tired, Jamie wrapped her in his shirt and tied it over his back, saying, "She's gonna get beat if she shits on me."

I prayed the little creature would not.

By the time we reached home it was nearly time for Jamie to catch the supply train back to camp, so while he settled the little pig in the hog lot I bundled a set of his clean clothes and brought him a nice drink of water from the springhouse. After he left, I poured a bucketful of water in the v-shaped pig trough he'd made of boards, then leaned over the fence and watched her drink. I didn't know what to feed her, because my uncle had not raised pigs, but Jamie said she'd eat about anything. He said wild pigs got along on roots and all kinds of greens and bugs. I pulled the roots of the cut cabbages, but she didn't seem interested in those. I also gave her some of the half-dead bean plants and a heel of stale bread. She ate the bread.

That evening she whined so pitifully that I carried her to the house and set her on my lap. She seemed to like that, and as the sun went down I stroked her fat belly and scratched her ears and let her eat a morsel of cornbread from my hand. "Nellie," I said. "You're my Nellie." I fell asleep like that and when I woke she was snoring. Not wanting to find my way to the hog lot in the dark, I carried her inside and let her sleep beside me on the bed.

At times that week I wished I was anywhere but here. Other days seemed nearly perfect, watching the leaves turn from green to red and yellow, Nellie nearby as I stitched the second quilt, shredded the cabbages and salted them in a crock. I was proud when she left me to explore the clearing and when she returned to sit with me on the porch. I was careful to feed her only in the hog lot, so she'd be used to it when Jamie came home. Like me, she liked cornmeal mush.

Saturday afternoon and Sunday morning Jamie and I devoted almost every waking hour to cutting wood, for he did not want me to be cold in the winter ahead. Wood warmed a person twice, he said, once when it was cut and again when it was burned. He wielded the ax and saw and showed me how to use the hatchet to split off slivers of wood for kindling. I didn't want to think about winter, but I vowed to be strong for him.

Hoping we'd go to town soon, each evening the next week I worked on another letter to my family, describing our progress and stressing Jamie's hard work and concern for my welfare. I wrote everything slowly after much consideration, afraid my family might misinterpret. I did not describe my loneliness, nor how it felt to be adored by Jamie Long.

When we were together, I believed those hours would sustain me forever, the memory of his weary face brightening each time he jumped off the log train, how he stopped and looked at me in the midst of his work, how tenderly he rested his cheek to mine.

The growing familiarity and freedom of his body beside me in the night. Was this worth everything? I thought it was. I couldn't write those things to my family.

Every Friday morning I woke up excited, thinking of Jamie's return, but on a Friday in early September I felt an unusual burst of energy and positive feeling. Tomorrow we were to go to town. The weather had been lovely, too, perfect for any kind of work. But in the night I woke up, very hot and sick to my stomach. About to throw up, I staggered outside to lean over the porch, and misjudging my location in the dark, I stepped over the edge to the ground, twisting my ankle. I screamed, but there was no one to hear or help. I turned to my side and retched and spit until I was faint. My ankle wouldn't bear my weight, and the night was cold and the ground was damp. I crawled to the step and back into the cabin.

I slept and woke, hot and thirsty, and with the broom handle for a cane, got out of bed and hopped to the water pitcher. Through the window I saw the drifting fog and behind it, a train stopped on the tracks and passengers boarding with their boxes and bags. Opening the window, I called, "Wait." The engineer waved. But my ankle hurt and I could not find my valise, and the train left without me. My first awareness in the morning was the despair of being forgotten and left, but then I knew the train had been a dream. There were no other people here.

I felt slightly better when I heard the afternoon log train, but my throat was raw from throwing up, and I was exhausted from trying to do anything with only one good leg. Even so, I hopped to the doorway and waved as Jamie leaped to the ground and trudged toward me, his sack of clothes over his shoulder. His face was angry and red.

Drawing near, he said, "Don't be waving like that; you don't know what kind of men them is."

What kind of men? I thought the men on the flatcar were his friends. I tried to speak but mixed my words with gasps and sobs.

"May Rose! What now? Stop that and talk plain."

I sniffed back the moisture dripping from my nose. "I wasn't waving at those men, I was waving at you. And there's no dinner made."

He brushed past me into the house. "And you're still in your nightdress?"

I hopped inside and sat on the bed. "Jamie, I've been sick. And I've hurt my ankle. I'm sorry to be so clumsy."

At once his face and tone changed. "Oh, dearie, I'm sorry." He grabbed me in a hug that nearly pulled me over. "You can't walk? We were going to town today."

I shook my head, holding on.

He lifted a burlap bag from the nail where it hung. "I better get on, then," he said.

"You're going without me? So soon?"

"If I don't go now I won't get back before dark. You can't go, can you?" He gave me a quick kiss. "I'll get what we need."

I didn't let myself cry again until he left. Then I hobbled around, spreading up the bed, putting beans and potatoes to cook with a bit of ham, wishing he'd put off the trip until I could go.

The days had become shorter, and it was twilight when he emerged from the forest path, bent with a heavy load. "Look what I found," he said, laying his bundles on our table. From one of the sellers in the street he'd bought a knitted cap for himself and wool coats for both of us. Mine reached to my ankles and was too broad in the shoulders, but it was warm and had only a few moth holes.

He'd also bought a shotgun, a heavy double-barreled thing, and of this he seemed most proud. "Tomorrow I'll show you how to use it," he said.

He'd eaten a sausage and a sweet pie in town, so he didn't want the meal I'd cooked, but he sat at the table for a cup of coffee. "I saw Russell in town, and here's the best news. If it don't rain Monday, he'll bring up some supplies I ordered."

"Will you be here when he comes?"

"Not on a Monday, no. But ain't you glad?"

"Of course," I said.

"Don't worry, he won't charge us nothing. You'll have a whole side of bacon, cornmeal, dried beans, and a sack of cracked corn for the chickens."

It was no time to be particular about who delivered things we needed so badly. I envied women who lived in town and walked to the store any time they pleased.

The next day Jamie shaved the branches from a forked tree limb to create a crutch. I doubted I'd need the crutch very long, because the swelling of my ankle was already going down, and I was starting to put a little weight on that foot.

Then he showed me how to clean, load, and fire the shotgun, which was almost too heavy to hold. He was standing behind me when I pulled the triggers, and he caught me before the recoil pushed me to the ground.

Then he laughed. "Holy hell! I never thought you'd try to pull both triggers at once. You got strong fingers, sweet pea, but next time, brace yourself before you fire. And just one barrel at a time, so you'll have the next one ready if you need it!"

How was I to know? And was I supposed to relax now, or should I be more worried and alert because he thought I'd need a gun?

<h1 style="text-align:center">CHAPTER 15</h1>

I made use of the gun the very next day. My sprained ankle had healed, and I'd started to cut down the dead garden plants. I was taking a rest on the porch step with a cup of water, watching Nellie root for acorns at the edge of the clearing, when a squawking fuss among the chickens turned my gaze toward the tracks. They were scattering in all directions, and a strange man was holding one by a leg. I'd worried about protecting the chicks and hens from hawks and owls, foxes, coyotes, raccoons, dogs and other animals, but I hadn't considered a human thief.

I yelled, but he tucked the chicken into a burlap bag without looking up.

Jamie had left the shotgun against the wall, just inside the door. It took two seconds to raise it to my shoulder and pull back both hammers. I yelled again, "Drop it or I'll shoot!"

He stopped but did not drop the bag. I hurried into the yard, angry enough to go closer for a better shot. He looked faded and rough, like all the workmen I'd seen on the log trains. He let the bag fall to the ground. I watched the chicken spurt away.

"Didn't know nobody lived here," he said. "You can put that gun down. I ain't gonna hurt nothing."

I braced my feet as Jamie had directed, but my arms were tense and near to shaking with the weight of the shotgun. "You're a liar and a thief. Get yourself gone before my husband comes back. He'll not give you a chance to get away!"

The thief hesitated, glanced around the clearing, threw up his hands and turned toward the tracks. I followed as far as the track, and though the gun strained my neck and shoulders, I kept it raised as he walked downhill. I didn't lower it until he disappeared around a curve.

After that, I was too weak to do anything, and I spent the next hour in the cabin with the bar on the door. He might come back. There might be others. And what might happen if I dropped him or someone else to the ground, shot full of holes and bleeding? The probabilities made me sick.

I kept looking at the shotgun propped by the door, and when I heard a thump on the porch floor I grabbed the gun and peered out the window. Then I set the gun down and opened the door. A horse stood by the porch. Russell dropped another sack, looked up and mumbled, "The rest is out there by the hog lot. Tell Jamie I'll be here on Saturday."

He was coming again on Saturday? "Stay and have a bite to eat," I said.

"I'll get a drink at the springhouse and be gone." He looked around. "I guess this place ain't so bad."

"Jamie has worked hard," I said.

Russell stared at the wild Morning Glory vine I'd pulled up in the garden and re-planted at the corner of the porch. In the garden it had wrapped itself around cornstalks—now it vined up a roof support. He set another bag, this one ragged and nearly empty, beside the others. "This here is from home."

"I'm surely grateful," I said. The bag held a few dozen apples, red ones. "I'll make a pie for Saturday when you're here."

Russell didn't nod or say anything else, but oddly, his brief visit went a long way toward easing my morning's fears. It would be something new, having him here with Jamie and me on Saturday, and though I was still half afraid of him, I looked forward to having a guest.

* * *

My four little chicks proved to be two hens and two roosters, and there was a good chance the hens would produce new broods in the spring, if I could keep them alive till then. Each evening I shelled a few grains of corn in the chicken coop to draw them inside, then locked them in for the night. Next year, if I had a bigger flock, I'd need a much larger corn patch.

Jamie had cut the corn stalks and we'd tied them in six shocks with the ears husked so they'd continue to dry. The ears had filled out nicely, but there weren't many, certainly not enough to feed Nellie all winter, nor the chickens either. She'd been ranging farther and farther under the trees, eating acorns, and she was getting fat. That week I joined her in the woods, scooping acorns with a bucket and dumping them in a bin in her house, a small provision against a time when the forest floor would be covered with snow.

I thought all week about whether or not to tell Jamie about the thief, and finally decided there'd be no benefit in it. He'd be angry, but he'd say lots of people were on their own, like me, and we all needed to keep a look out.

I did tell Jamie about his brother's visit. "Russell said he's coming today. Did you know?"

He shook his head. "Did he say what for?"

"Maybe just to visit?"

Jamie laughed. "Likely he wants something."

Jamie was digging a winter pit for our potatoes, and I'd just taken the pie from the oven when Russell arrived, his horse carrying bundles of thin wooden strips. Jamie stopped digging and walked to the chicken house, where Russell was unloading the bundles on his horse. The next time I looked out, the two of them were coming from the woods, carrying large rocks. They did that for more than an hour, laying the rocks near the chicken house. It looked to me like Russell had come to build something, but no one had said what it was to be.

I'd let my second crop of runner beans dry on the vines, then had pulled the plants and laid them on the roof of Nellie's house. To keep myself busy in a place where I could see Jamie, I dragged the vines to the porch. Then I sat on the step and pulled off the pods, shooing Nellie away. She could eat the vines, but I intended to hang the dry pods inside for wintertime meals. While I worked I watched Jamie and Russell begin a narrow addition to the chicken house, a slatted room for corn. I could see it might be fine for the future, but this year our corn would barely cover the floor. I couldn't hear what they said, but I heard the tone of their voices, often raised in anger.

After lunch, Russell left for home, and I had Jamie to myself again. Between them, they'd devoured the pie.

"The old fool didn't ask if I wanted a corn crib, just went ahead and started it. And it all had to be done his way," Jamie said.

The crib was not even half finished, but I admired it. They'd built a floor on pillars of rock topped with squares of tin. Jamie said the tin was to keep rats from climbing up the sides. I didn't ask if he thought Russell would charge him for the wood and tin he'd brought. If Jamie had thanked his brother, he'd done it where I couldn't hear.

"We're gonna have to put up with him next Saturday," Jamie said. "He's just like Pa, thinks I can't do nothing on my own."

"He admires what you've accomplished here," I said.

"Russell said that?"

"He said it kind of to himself. It was something like, 'The place looks good'."

Secretly, I wished Russell lived closer. It would be good to know I could go somewhere if I needed help. He might be dependable, even though he didn't like me.

Russell showed up again the next Saturday and was already working on the crib when Jamie jumped from the log train.

"Can't get rid of him, I guess," Jamie said. "You better go ahead and bury the potatoes so I can help on the crib."

I'd already buried the potatoes, spreading them in the pit between layers of dirt and dried grass. I'd also finished cutting down the garden and had opened the gate so Nellie could root there. My chickens had followed her, pecking bugs from the dirt she turned over.

"Maybe there's something I can do to help you and Russell," I said.

"Maybe there is, but he won't like you hanging around."

Disappointed, I returned to the house.

Jamie and Russell appeared to get along better that day, and when I fed them dinner Russell seemed almost congenial, though still he said nothing to me. There'd been enough apples for another pie, and this time I put aside a small slice for myself before setting the pie on the table. Since we had only two chairs, I ate my beans, bread, and pie later.

After Russell left, Jamie and I sat on the porch step. Nellie seemed wary of Jamie and kept her distance when he was home. Instead of coming to lie beside me, she spread out in her hog lot.

"That pig's near to butchering size," Jamie said.

A shock went through me. "She's not for butchering."

"Not right away, but in a couple of months. Like some fine Saturday in December. Russell will come and help."

"No."

"No? You don't want Russell to help?"

"No, we'll not butcher the pig." My voice shook. I'm keeping her. We'll raise our own pigs. That's why we got a sow, right?"

He put his arm around my shoulders. "Sure, but we'd have to take her someplace to get bred. That'd be hard to do. Right now you need meat for winter; remember, when the snow comes we might not get to town. Russell's got a sausage grinder. I'll fix a place in the shed to hang the hams."

I'd never felt so insistent about anything. "Not Nellie."

"Who's Nellie?"

"My pig. She's not for butchering."

"*Your* pig? It wasn't smart to give her a name."

I got up and paced in front of the porch. "You don't know what it's like to be here alone. You see people every day, work with them, talk to them. Maybe you don't like many of them, maybe not even one, but to me it's worse, seeing no one at all."

"Calm down, now," he said. "Lots of people live alone and hardly ever see a soul. Russell gets along."

"Russell? I'm not like Russell and you're not, either. You wouldn't like it, living here by yourself. I need Nellie."

"You need a pig!" He laughed.

"I need somebody."

"A pig don't talk," he said.

"She's a comfort." I hated myself for crying, certain it made me look weak, certain that was how Jamie thought of me.

"Get hold of yourself, May Rose. You know I want what's best for you."

I said no more. He might want the best, but I couldn't believe he was the only one who knew what the best was.

We did not talk about Nellie again until the next day, when he was preparing to leave for the camp. "Don't be mad," he said.

"If you butcher Nellie, I think I'll die."

"Don't be a fool," he said.

"Jamie, I'll starve before…" I couldn't say it.

"You'll change your mind when you get hungry."

"I won't."

He tried to kiss me goodbye, but I kept my lips closed and still.

* * *

That week I suffered from regret as well as from my usual loneliness. At times I'd doubted Jamie's decisions, but I'd never openly opposed him, and until the issue of Nellie, I'd never argued. I still felt a hard place in my middle, just thinking of his suggestion, and with Nellie snuggled on the porch beside me when I rested from work, I knew I was right.

I had to make him change his mind, but what would I do if he didn't?

A week apart was not quite enough to make us forget our disagreement, and the next Saturday our greeting was strained. "Going to Russell's," he said, soon after depositing his bag of dirty clothes on the cabin floor.

"Me too?"

"Not this time."

"Will you be back tonight or tomorrow?"

"Tomorrow," he said.

Just like that, he was gone, and he'd taken the shotgun. I hated this division between us, but I could not give in.

Jamie returned on Sunday just in time to catch the supply train back to camp. He picked up his bag of clean clothes. "Me and Russell got a deer," he said. "He'll dress it out and bring your half over. If you don't know how to cut it up and dry the meat, ask him."

That evening when Nellie came to be let into the cabin, I said, "I think maybe you're safe." But maybe only for a while.

CHAPTER 16

A t times I enjoyed the solitude. My time was my own, and as often as possible when the autumn days were fine I lay in the grass of the clearing and absorbed the heat of the sun, as though storing up for the cold ahead.

With no one to see or tell me what to do, I had abundant time to think, and when I felt at peace, I reflected that my trials here were nothing in comparison to Jamie's hard labor. Surely my fears were no greater than his concern for me.

Every time he came home, I forgot about my days and nights alone. There'd never been anything in my world like this man who teased me, kissed me, sang to me. I loved to help with his bath, cut his hair, button his shirt. Everything he did seemed designed to please me.

He exhausted himself cutting and stacking wood. "I want to do better," he said, "because you are perfect."

I worked harder, trying to be perfect, because he thought I was.

When he complained about his work in the camp, I begged him to quit the company. "A man has to prove himself with men," he said. "That's what I'm doing. Someday I'll be a boss."

"And then you'll like the work."

He laughed. "I think the bosses hates it too, 'cause they're mean as hell."

I laughed too, though I was sad that so many people hated their work. When he spoke of men who seemed friendly, I asked, "Do you have special friends?"

"My pretty little wife is my special friend," he said. "But men, no. Men ain't like women, flocking together like hens. There's some in camp I respect and some I hate. It's best to be the same to all. The men likes my songs and my stories. If I don't like somebody I do my best to keep my mouth shut."

I hoped Jamie was not aiming too high, wanting to be a boss, when he'd worked for the company only a few months. Whenever I felt a twinge of wanting, I told myself a person who wanted too much would never be satisfied.

I sharpened the old man's meat knives, wondering if I'd be able to figure out how to cut up and preserve the deer, but weeks passed before Russell brought it, and then he'd cut, smoked, and dried strips of it for us. "Did your'n along with mine," he mumbled. "Easier that way."

Easier than showing me or having to talk with me, I was sure. He'd smoked and salted the hindquarters, and I hung my portion from a hook in the corner of the cabin.

Another time I went out in the morning and found a burlap bag full of apples and another of dried corn on the porch. I added the corn to our meager harvest in the corn crib, then spent the week cutting and drying the apples.

Jamie was happy when he came home and saw the deer meat, the corn in the crib and the dried apples hanging on the cabin walls.

"It might just do," Jamie said. "We've made a good start. Someday we'll go where it ain't so hard to get along."

Excited, I told him then about the letter I'd written to my uncle. "Sure," he said. "We might go to North Dakota or we might go somewhere else, soon as the time is right."

I knew we wouldn't move away now, with winter on the way,

but I wondered if there might be a letter waiting for me in Winkler. Cautiously I asked, "Could we go down to town next Saturday?"

"That'll depend," he said.

We didn't go to town the next Saturday. Jamie fell asleep as soon as he got home but woke for supper. That night he sang as we danced around the table. After that we slept in a heat of satisfaction.

Sunday the wind brought a few flakes of snow and Jamie piled more wood behind the cabin and carried in a load of kindling. Before running to jump on the train he said, "I'll dream of you until I see you again. Dream of me."

Through the week I not only dreamed, I thought of him almost every moment. He'd made himself part of me, along with everything I'd touched in this place, and it all seemed good. I loved the scent of the earth after a rain, the murmur of my chickens as they settled for the night, the brush of air through the trees. I loved watching the changing sky.

I realized that to live alone, a woman had to be attuned to everything around her. She also needed to be primed for change.

A year ago I hadn't met Jamie and I'd never been anywhere. Who could say what another year might bring? In my dreams I saw a house in town, a house with neighbors and friends. In my dreams I saw children.

I had to believe this time would end and something better would begin. I would make it so.

    * * *

DEAR READER

Thank you for reading *For the Love of Jamie Long*. The story of May Rose's life continues in the 14 books of The Mountain Women Series, starting with *The Girl on the Mountain*. You can read the first chapters of all these books on my website, www.carol ervin.com.

I hope you enjoyed this story, and I hope you will share the title with your friends. Please leave a rating or review on Amazon or Facebook or other sites to help readers find the kind of books they like.

Carol Ervin

GIRL ON THE MOUNTAIN
BOOK 1 OF THE MOUNTAIN WOMEN SERIES

In 1899, an abandoned young wife and a homeless girl team up to survive in a remote sawmill town in the Appalachian Mountains.

The young woman's name is May Rose Long, but in the town where she seeks refuge, she's slandered as "the girl on the mountain." With no money and no resources other than her pet sow's litter of pigs, she must find safe shelter and respectable work.

The company doctor wants to help, but he's married, and his interest is personal. The company manager offers work, but his concern for May Rose may not be proper. Then there's Suzie, operator of the brothel, who'd gladly welcome both her and the girl. As May Rose struggles to earn her keep, her troubles seem directed by others.

Soon an accident leaves the town in desperate straits. Through it all, she must protect herself and the girl who sleeps with a doll clutched tight and a knife under her pillow.

The story of May Rose and Wanda is the first book in the Mountain Women Series, bringing to life the struggles and triumphs, friendships, and families of women in a small West Virginia town in the early 1900s.

"An emotionally gripping and powerful novel you won't be able to put down!" — Goodreads reviewer

ABOUT THE AUTHOR

I've been lucky. Years ago, I wanted to live on a farm, and my husband said "Let's do it." When personal computers were introduced, I wanted to know about them and own one, and lucky me, the school where I taught offered a course in Basic. When we bought our first computer, I discovered the writer's best friend--word processing. Before that, I could not write without crossing out most of a typewritten or handwritten page, and progress seemed impossible. When I wanted to shift from teaching to writing, the first Macintosh computers came out, and I was lucky enough to have, along with technical and business writing, the first "desktop publishing" service in my area. And when finally I had the leisure to give a lot of time to a novel, my husband didn't merely tolerate my commitment, he encouraged it.

Inspiration for the Mountain Women series came first from the mountain wilderness, both beautiful and challenging for those who live there. I appreciated accounts of early 20th century life and industry, the forerunners of today's technology and culture. When I read Roy B. Clarkson's non-fiction account of lumbering in West Virginia, (Tumult on the Mountain, 1964, McClain Printing Co., Parsons, WV), with more than 250 photos of giant trees, loggers, sawmills, trains, and towns, I found the setting for the first book in the series. Finally, I was inspired by men and women of previous generations who faced difficulties unknown today. Researching and writing these novels, I have felt closer to the lives of grandparents I never knew.

Learn more about author Carol Ervin at http://www.carol ervin.com

facebook.com/carolervin.author
bookbub.com/authors/carol-ervin

Other Novels

Ridgetop

Dell Zero

ACKNOWLEDGMENTS

Once again I'm grateful to these early readers for their encouragement and helpful suggestions for this book: June Dickenson and Aimee Ay.

You're the best!